THE KINDRED HERITAGE

Novels by Dennis Bowen

International Thriller Series

THE WATER DIAMONDS
Book 1

THE BLACKSTONE PERFECTION
Book 2

THE CRYSTAL SEDUCTION
Book 3

THE REDROCK QUARANTINE
Book 4

THE FINAL MASQUERADE
Book 5

THE VIRTUE TRANSITION
Book 6

THE JASMINE NEGATIVE
Book 7

THE GOSPEL LABYRINTH
Book 8

The Backstory Files

STONES
Book 1

THE KINDRED HERITAGE

Dennis Bowen

ISBN: 978-1-7360262-5-0

www.facebook.com/DennisBowenThrillers

www.twitter.com/DBowenThrillers

www.DennisBowen.com

Book Interior Design by 52 Novels

ACKNOWLEDGMENTS

At the risk of repeating myself, thank you to the readers worldwide who have immersed themselves in my *International Thriller Series*. While I create the intrigues that span the globe and enjoy every minute of it, in the end, I write these novels for you and your enjoyment. It's really that simple.

As with *The Water Diamonds, The Blackstone Perfection, The Crystal Seduction, The Redrock Quarantine, The Final Masquerade, The Virtue Transition, The Jasmine Negative*, and *The Gospel Labyrinth*, my appreciation and gratitude goes out to those who offered suggestions and encouragement during the writing of *The Kindred Heritage*.

I express appreciation to my fabulous editor, Laura Taylor. She has provided the editing prowess to insure a quality presentation for this series and for STONES, the initial offering of *The Backstory Files*.

As in life, each successive endeavor—such as writing a series of novels—is built on what came before. Any errors or omissions in *The Kindred Heritage* I claim as my own.

I extend my gratitude to family members and friends for their support, and to former colleagues, some of whom offered up their lives in the service of this great country, and whose presence in my life gives my International Thriller Series its noted sense of reality. Thank you to all.

Dennis Bowen

CHAPTER 1

It wasn't the explosion that got their attention.

The rising mushroom cloud seemed far away. But the people running, screaming through the streets were near.

The dropped jaws said it all.

"That's me!"

"And me!"

The Crayles gasped.

The visual, on the highest definition flat screen available to the CIA, was stark.

The couple running on the treacherous cobblestones through the ancient city was them. Their faces, their experiences seemed absolutely real.

Crayle, hunched forward and breathing hard, forced himself to sit back and assess.

The visual remained relentless. It morphed to a view his own eyes would have in that circumstance.

"That's not me!"

"But it is!"

"It never happened!"

"It's real."

"They can create reality. I'm smelling S & T."

"S and T? Micmac works with them."

Crayle grabbed his Smartphone.

The TV feed switched to another covert team member.

"Micmac!"

The former SEAL, underwater demolitions, and weapons expert. And adjunct inventor for the CIA's Science and Technology Directorate.

The man raced into view from a dark alley. Right behind him, his wife. Borrowed FBI Agent, Phoebe.

Seconds later, another alley coughed up Lenny and Alona.

The entire team rendered in a stark, but nonexistent reality.

CHAPTER 2

The video fantasy jumped to a solo Crayle.

He ran full tilt down the Hall of Mirrors.

The crunch of the myriad shards of shattered glass dealt him the reality. Most would have given up at the passageway's end now far behind. Or would have stepped carefully forward in order not to rupture their feet. Certainly not when wearing nothing on them but his signature ECCO sandals.

He caught a glimpse of himself to one side as he passed. A large mirror fragment that survived the blast.

Magus Crayle.

Director of Central Intelligence-elect. Running like he was twenty.

Not the sunset years neophyte he'd recently become.

Noises from behind.

The crew of a secret society, black ops paramilitants chasing him rounded the corner. They let fly with their suite of AK-47s on full auto. Accuracy while running over broken glass took a beating.

To Crayle's benefit.

Typically, people run away from, or run to, something.

The Illuminé thugs were the *from*.

Up ahead was the *to*.

A miniature nuclear device. The last of its kind remaining.

Why, he wondered, did he always push untenable to new extremes?

He heard an outcry.

One of the men at the group's front had fallen. Sliced and diced unmercifully over his entire body.

Good. It slowed them down.

Just enough.

To his left, a door.

He gasped. There was a corollary to Murphy's Law. Any door necessary for survival … would be locked.

Not always.

The crème with gold trim portal opened with ease.

As he passed through, he heard an outcry in French from behind that his mind quickly translated as "*Excrement!*"

He didn't even know the language.

Locking the now closed door would be a waste of time against the AK-47s. He did it anyway.

Habit.

Quick across the room, likewise heavy with gold trim on cream-colored walls. It wasn't like he was in the Palace of Versailles or anything. Actually, he transited the replica rebuilt after Pattie's bomb demolished the original.

He yanked open the far door.

The throne room.

He fully expected to find his old nemesis turned precious ally, Jean-Marc Lalumière.

And there he stood. All six-foot-six of him in his Louis XX regalia.

The second modern era King of France, following his father's untimely demise. At Pattie's hand. On coronation day.

The king, still in his twenties, regarded a display case next to his non-replica Louis XIV desk.

Still well aware of the danger behind him, Crayle approached.

Jean-Marc lifted a trophy bowl from the case, and turned toward his anticipated guest.

"This just doesn't seem to fit." He extended his arms, proffering the silver metal vessel and its contents.

It was what Crayle had come for. Risked everything for. Saving lives of the innocent, and taking the lives of the guilty summed up his life as an off-the-books, Company operative.

Just this one last op before taking the helm.

He plucked the rugby ball from the trophy cup.

Five megatons of destruction resided in the so-called mini-nuke.

Like all the others before it, Made In China. This was the final one. Just then, the rattle of automatic gunfire assaulted the chamber.

The hit team had breached the locked door.

Crayle couldn't let them reassert ownership of the bomb. He seemed out of options. He pulled the nuclear device close.

Jean-Marc twisted, then tilted a period-appearing desk lamp with unique features. Its presentation and installation had been a special gift from American President Stones via the CIA's Science and Technology Directorate.

The young king's move caused the four corners of the lush carpet in the next room to shoot upwards, encapsulating the attack team.

The invisible wiring crisscrossed at the high ceiling, knotting itself. Pulling the killers into a lump made attempts to fire their weapons effectively fruitless.

"Watch this!" Jean-Marc advised with a grin.

Two now bare panels comprising the floor slid apart.

The carpet-corralled glom of would-be assassins plopped into a man-made tributary of the Seine River.

As if nothing abnormal had transpired, the panels slid closed.

"I wanted to replace that old carpet anyway," Jean-Marc said.

He then nodded toward the bathroom to his left.

Crayle knew what that meant.

His way out.

CHAPTER 3

Now, it was Hekka's turn.

She ran across the uneven ground as quickly as possible.

Her well-armed pursuers helped her with location by their incessant yelling, one to another.

She always stayed far enough ahead that a sight picture and pursuit ending shot could not be achieved.

The walls of the cliffs on either side converged ahead. Light that shone through an opening barely enough for a skinny person proved her only option. Turning back portended certain death.

Squeezing through the opening, she caught her breath, and stopped dead at the sight before her.

One more step, and she'd plunge 500 feet onto a dry river bed below.

Slight projections were now in view as the bluff continued on her right. They could provide the most meager of hand- and footholds. Her only choice.

Others might conclude she was doomed. Her husband would not. His faith in her abilities and determination surpassed unshakeable.

She pressed on.

Her moccasins allowed a feel of the outcroppings, no matter how miniscule. It seemed they'd signed on to keep her steady and safe as long as her fingers grasped at barely existent hand holds.

The shouting back to her right grew louder.

As Hekka Crayle glanced back, she knew that if just one of the killers passed through the mountain's constricted opening, she was a sitting duck. Or one sitting Serrano Indian duck.

Ahead, the semi-circular cliff face curved right.

Could she pass around the bend to safety in time?

The first killer to pass into view was one chosen because she was the thinnest.

She almost took a step too many that would have plunged her into the gorge below.

They locked eyes.

Hekka knew she was done for. With all her heart, she dreaded the outcome that would separate her forever from her beloved husband and their baby girl, Kianna. She knew one thing. She would not cry. The Serrano and Christian heavens were one, she was certain. They'd be together again. Some day.

But the only female of the assassination squad refused to fire. She couldn't.

She turned, yelling something through the narrow opening behind her.

Hekka heard shouting back. The word, even in a foreign language, meant "Shoot!"

As the woman made her case, she made a fatal error. She stepped back. As if to distance herself from the rest of the team. All men.

She lost her balance, and fell. Hollering her defiance until 500 feet and several seconds later, her outcries ended.

Hekka thought of crossing herself in the Roman Catholic manner, but decided against it.

She'd seen the troop of pursuers before at a distance. The men comprising the bulk of the killer team couldn't squeeze through the narrow opening to take the shot.

Minutes later she'd pulled herself along and looked in surprise at her good fortune.

A few feet ahead. The opening of a cave.

Since the foot and hand holds past its entrance diminished to near nonexistence, the choice to enter or not to enter was made for her.

In she went, smiling now that, just maybe, she'd be with her precious Magus. And yes, her baby Kianna. In this lifetime. Once again.

CHAPTER 4

After the video-induced heavy breathing of Crayle and his wife, it was Micmac and Phoebe MacKay's turn.

The two ran full speed around their respective corners. And banged into each other.

Their collective "Oof!" could be heard a distance away.

The blonde, positioning her Weaver-gripped Glock 30 with an upward tilt FBI posture, grazed her husband's forehead with the slide.

Micmac, his fist closed around a .40 caliber pistol held across his abdomen, nicked her lower rib.

In that instant, they spun to a back-to-back configuration.

"Where to now, my love?" she whispered.

"They're Illuminé. Whether the secret society still wishes us dead for specific purpose, or just in general, we don't know."

"Dead is dead. Purpose doesn't help. Do something!"

"We SEALS don't have time for your Agency's fancy, two-handed, short-gun techniques. So, with my free hand, I'll call Kimbel."

"Brilliant. The president can have a government team here by next week."

"Silly me."

The sounds outside made themselves felt.

The CIA safe house shook as multiple helicopters, loaded with secret society operatives, touched down.

"They're upping their game, Phoebs. Those sound like Apaches."

"My sport before joining the Crayle team was protecting federal witnesses, not recognizing military hardware. Let's blow this joint."

"I left my C-4 toys at home. Damn!"

"C'mon, Micmac. These safe houses have an exit strategy built in!"

They both turned, and chorused.

"The bathroom!"

Ten seconds later they were across the room and down a narrow hall.

Once inside the bathroom, the two supplied their CIA-requisite pubic hair credentials into the special urinal.

Before the assassination squad outside could break through the reinforced entry points, Phoebe and Micmac shot straight down into one of the CIA's signature, below-ground operational quarters. Their transport capsule struck bottom with a thud.

"That was about 300 feet. Just like back home." He referred to the covert hospital deep under a gravel quarry near Southern California's Big Bear Valley where all three team couples lived.

"Make that 100 meters," Phoebe corrected. "We're in Europe."

Now away from the safe house, they followed a metal-lined tunnel. To safety.

• • •

The assault team, finally having made its way inside, thoroughly searched the building.

"No one nowhere," one of them concluded in French.

They all shrugged.

The leader pointed at his crotch, and the bathroom.

He stepped through the bathroom door, but the transit module had not yet returned topside.

He fell, never to be seen again.

When three cohorts stepped inside the bathroom to see why he hadn't returned, they found it back to normal, but empty.

They returned to the others, and their senior man remarked in his best colloquial English. "Not there. Musta fell in."

They laughed. They shrugged. And they left.

CHAPTER 5

It was over. The heavy breathing and sweating complete. Time to assess the damage. Crayle started it off.

"One thing is abundantly clear. Not a second of these videos ever happened. Yet, they seemed real in every way. The renderings of each of our voices, physical appearances, and actions—our very personas, for Chrissakes—could fool anyone." All bodies, and all eyes, fixated on Micmac.

"Hey, it's not like I created this fake reality software. Uh, not like I worked on it full time. Uh ..."

Crayle glared. "This snake has to be returned to the pillow case before it bites us all."

Phoebe provided a quick nod. "Bites us on our collective ass!"

The Gadget Man, Micmac, refused to concede his latest effort. "But someone else will do it if we don't."

Crayle considered the apparently non-existent options. "It has to be developed carefully, and with incessant, contiguous containment. Full, ultra-Top Secret clearances. Then, a planned 'put it on the shelf until needed' operation that ensures there are no copies of the app. Finally, accessibility to it must be no less than the virtual equivalent of the president's so-called nuclear weapon football."

"Ack on that, Mag. I'll shift gears, develop the necessary protocols, and hold it all close to the vest. With regards to any help I'll need, …"

"Negats on the help, for now. You quarantine this sucker. When you've got a plan, it's you and I. No one else."

"Not even Kimbel?"

"Giving a president this kind of power—to have Grand Ayatollahs on artificial intelligence-generated video extolling the virtues of Israel, for example—might be too much temptation. Even for a genuinely good man like Kimbel."

"And we must remember. He won't always be America's president."

"Precisely, Hekka. I hereby proclaim this the Pandora Project. Micmac, be sure this nascent monster you've created stays in the box."

"Wilco, Mag. Will comply."

CHAPTER 6

With two Dassault Falcon jets available on short notice, it didn't take Magus Crayle long to reach his destination in Washington, D.C., and to make his way to the STIF, the Sound and Technology Isolated Facility situated deep beneath the White House. He could tell right away the president was borderline miffed.

"So, Mag, you told some displaced Persian you met in Mumbai, who wants to blow up Iran, that you'd deliver me as needed?" President Stones endured the ensuing couple of heart pounds. "I have enough trouble keeping my promises to the American people, and the rest of the planet, without you adding more … more … promises."

"But, I—"

"We don't have computers big enough to count the number of ways this could go wrong. I can see the headlines. PARTIAL-TERM PRESIDENT FLUSHED DOWN TOILET BY CIA DCI HE RECENTLY APPOINTED.

"I didn't *really* promise your help."

Stones calmed slightly. "You didn't?"

Crayle's poker face didn't budge. He dwelled on the positive potential.

The man glaring at him re-escalated the rhetoric. "If we didn't have a system in place at the NSA to scan all the country's emails in real time ... and yank all the bad stuff, the previous headline would by preceded by U.S. PRESIDENT STONES AUTHORIZED THIRD PARTY OVERTHROW OF IRAN ... USING SMALL NUCLEAR DEVICES ... OBTAINED FROM CHINA!"

Crayle held up his hands. Palms forward. "Kimbel! I've got this!"

Stones sat back. "Oh! Swell! I can see myself floating out to sea with the rest of the political sewage saying, *Mag had this*."

"I suppose trust me isn't going to work here."

"Ha!"

"Look. Give me 24. I'll have a plan. You'll love it. It'll be a winner. The press'll say, STONES ASSURED OF A SECOND TERM. You won't even have to mention my name," Crayle said with a smile.

Head bowed, the normally upbeat Stones sat with both hands pressed against his forehead. He looked up. "Twenty-four. Here. Tomorrow. And remember. Your job is to stop the world's mega-goons from blowing it up. Not help them do it."

Crayle initiated a "My mission, should I choose to accept it ..." response.

Stones allayed that with hands pushed his way. "Go!"

The president's favorite spy, and likely his best friend, stood outside the STIF in three seconds. With the door closed, he managed his second smile of the encounter. He knew. It'd be a long 24.

• • •

Precisely 24 hours later, Stones sat ensconced in the STIF once again. Crayle, characteristically prompt if nothing else, hadn't arrived with his plan.

Susanna, the president's top and most trusted aid, and former Mossad operative, poked her head in the door. "Got comms from

Mr. Crayle. Couldn't reach you in the STIF." She handed him a folded paper.

President Stones read it.

He couldn't believe it.

"He went where!"

CHAPTER 7

The previous Grand Ayatollah, leader of Iran, Dohreihmi Fahsolah was officially deceased. Kept from the public, it turned out the former leader was an atheist member of the secret society, Illuminé, had kids, and a wife. And it also turned out, she was Zoroastrian, the prime religion of ancient Persia.

His successor, the new and current Grand Ayatollah leader of Iran, Rafsan Jahni, observed the children. No matter how deadly his duties became, one's kids could bring even the most hearty and strong man to weakness. Another episode for those romance writers of the world. Such as his primary wife.

She stepped by him quickly to grab a child precariously perched on a 1960s vintage console stereo. Funny how things went. The government would pay citizens to assemble in a public square, and chant, "Down with America," while those at the top of the Iranian power structure coveted and proudly displayed any artifacts obtained from that country. Indeed, a great country.

So that was it. The now-deceased, Dohreihmi Fahsolah, had produced but two children by his first wife and his fourteenth wife, respectively. Tee, the boy, and a beautiful little girl given his own nickname, Doh. She'd even chosen her first song from the English language. "Doh, a doe, a female deer ..."

An epiphany occurred to the cleric. Allah created a cycle of birth and death so he, the Great One, could enjoy the children. And there would always be new ones. He'd even created one in his own image, and followed the child for years. But that brought Islam and Christianity together, didn't it."

The Grand Ayatollah sat back to consider the bond of the other two religions.

"Oh, my God," the Christians would say. And the Jews. "Oh, my God!"

How in the world could two religions be divided by a common God?

His mind led him elsewhere.

It was not long ago that he and his three cohorts had assassinated Grand Ayatollah Fahsolah in his own subterranean replica of the Roman Forum.

The former leader of Iran's replacement, also a Grand Ayatollah, addressed the other two members of the country's leadership circle. They'd waited patiently.

"We are besieged by the American, President Stones. The tariffs and other punishments throttle our economy. Our lifeblood, oil, cannot be sold anywhere."

His second in command, referred to by him as Number Two, just had to interrupt. "But it is needed worldwide."

"Stones has declared that anyone buying it would be complicit, equally guilty, and due to suffer the selfsame sanctions."

"Selfsame? Fancy English. You spent too many years in The Great Devil America university."

"My school, Arizona State, is famous for its sports teams. You are well informed regarding their mascots. The Sun Devils, as it were. How did you know?"

"I ... I ..."

"Wax quiescent, my friend." The room became very quiescent.

The third man raised his hand just enough to be noticed. "From the Quds Force, our domestic intelligence indicates that the Iranian serfs, about 90% of the society, are close to full scale revolt against us. We cannot kill them all. We cannot even put them all in prison."

The second in command, the idea man, just couldn't shut up. "Simple. Build more prisons. The builders, as well as all of their relatives and friends, will feel the fear."

"If not, we end up with the 10%, or fewer, of our ruling class having to do all of the country's work. It conflicts with our group narcissism."

"Narcissism. The inability to care about anyone but oneself." He nodded. "You're right."

"The other extreme solution has us divorcing our monetary, special operations, and intelligence support from the West-designated Islamic terrorist organizations. Our proxies throughout the Middle East."

"They would turn on us if we did."

"It gets worse. In order to make nice with the Americans, we'd be forced to pay young Iranians to shout *Up With America* rather than the opposite."

"Hardly acceptable."

The Quds head couldn't help but intercede on the two-way conversation. He'd avoided speaking in this forum unless absolutely necessary.

"There is a third option. Perhaps more acceptable ..."

That caught the leader's attention. A better idea was fine. And, if it went wrong, there would be someone else to blame other than the Grand Ayatollah. A scapegoat. "Tell us."

"When our Arab forebears conquered and subjugated the Persians and their empire, they went after the Zoroastrian majority. The rulers of the day."

"Let me get the substance of what you suggest," followed the Iranian leader. "We scapegoat the Zoros, who to this day remain in

Iran, blaming them for the hard times. Surely we can claim that Allah has been punishing us for not recognizing and dealing with their threat to his dominance. He is, after all, the One God. The Only God."

"Yes. But what of the Zoros expatriated, who have taken up as far away as India? Mumbai, for example. Our assault on domestic Zoros could rally the foreign ones, some of whom have attained great wealth, against us."

"What could such a small number possibly do?"

"Enough to think about."

The Quds head punctuated the obvious end-of-session by mounting a stage behind them as the curtains were drawn. There was the band he'd created as a sideline, indicating his obsession with Western Rock and Roll. He strapped on his certified-iconic, red Gibson ES-335 guitar, and launched into a rocking parody rendition of a Chuck Berry classic. *Jahni B. Goode.*

CHAPTER 8

The Grand Ayatollah leader of Iran, his Number Two Grand Ayatollah, religious liaison to the Islamic Revolutionary Guard Corps, IRGC, and Grand Ayatollah Number Three, religious liaison to the Quds Force, were at it again.

It was a new day. The stupor from the band and partying wore off. Alcohol secreted into a punch bowl only accessible to the Grand Ayatollahs indicated a loosening of Islamic fundamentalist constraints on behavior. It was one of the unintended outcomes of the recent B Summit of Middle Eastern top clerics held recently by American Magus Crayle in Casablanca.

Iran's leader, the Grandest Ayatollah and surely Number One, addressed religious leaders Number Two and Number Three once again. Number Two served as religious coordinator to the IRGC, the role of which was to preserve the Islamic revolution of 1979. Number Three filled the role of religious liaison to the Quds Force, the latter group utilizing the capabilities of a combination special operations command and CIA to support non-state, terrorist actors in foreign countries.

"We've had strong, indelible ties to Russia for decades. What is our current status with the new leadership?"

Having already conferred during the previous night's party with Number Three on the subject, the Number Two responded. "Czarina Anastasia is fully in charge of Russia. As you know, a small nuclear device was transported via our country. She saw to its deployment in Moscow's Red Square. At the tomb of Vladimir Lenin."

"Transported there from our homeland in the casket of the other Vladimir, the final president of the Russian Federation. Placed next to the other."

"In a way, the Czarina took out two Vladimirs for the price of one." Number Three laughed.

The leader ignored the lame joke. "What is not funny is that the immense financial support we've received from the Russians over the years seems to have dried up. What does our premiere espionage resource in that country have to say, Number Three?"

"As we all know, Russia's use for us isn't over oil reserves. It has plenty of its own. The 2015 agreement we had with the West allowed us a nuclear arsenal by 2025."

"Did our resource let on what the Russians expected us to do with those weapons, once developed?"

"He did. Suitably bribed with a large sum of our money, he divulged that the Russians intended to use us as a nuclear proxy, should the need arise."

The leader made the obvious observation, signified by a nod. "Just so."

Number Two supplied the downside. "And any and all like-kind retaliation would come down on Iran, not their country."

"They conveniently see it as a win-win. Their rationale is that we are a Muslim country. That we all want to die fighting the demons of the world. Our path to Paradise."

"Did you inform the resource that, no, we don't all want to die?"

"Not yet."

"He's here?"

"He is."

"Where is their new leader, the Czarina Anastasia, on our agreement?"

"She's been quite busy. And, according to the resource, wants to end the relationship. He says she's cozied up to the American president. And a particular member of the CIA."

"Cozied up?"

"Just shy of sex, the resource says."

"It would seem that her charms and her appetite are slipping. She has a reputation for being the second—and third, fourth, and so on—coming of Catherine The Great."

"I wouldn't know, in a direct sense, about this czarina's proclivities." Number Three did know, however, of the leader's sampling thereof. He wisely excluded that fact from the conversation.

"Well, see that our resource is fully satisfied in the appropriate manner, and send him home. We need him there, not here, to keep his ear to the ground. A now and then R & R here in Tehran is fine, but keep it brief. Okay?"

The Number Two responded for himself and the Number Three. "As you command, Sire."

The pair slowly bowed, then made their way out.

CHAPTER 9

She didn't get out much. As usual, the czarina and leader of Russia resided in her residence, thanks to the one-time leader of Russia, Catherine the Great.

Anastasia sat up in bed in her Saint Petersburg palace, unaware of the activities in the Iranian capitol. She'd been busy with Russian affairs of state which, to her, meant sex.

She mulled over her most recent accomplishment.

The czarina had just issued an edict that Russian Orthodoxy was back. It was now the official state religion. It was time that the morality supplied by the Creator displace the more earthy and corrupt morality dictated previously by the Communists. The rules wouldn't apply to the sovereign, no matter who dreamt them up. Done with that, she thought of the Parsi Rustom in Mumbai, India. How he'd enabled her nuclear takedown of all material opposition. She would bed him someday. If she hadn't already. Too many to remember. She smiled.

Raspi, just returned from Tehran, and her number one advisor and confidant, broke her reverie as he barged into her bedchamber. He waved a handful of papers written in Cyrillic.

"We've done it! Our very own psy-op! We blamed the residual Communists for the Moscow bombing!"

No questions, he moved on. "Surely, they attended Vladimir's lying in state as a tribute, but realized their political aspirations were forever like the Vladimirs. Dead. Using one of Russia's multitude of nuclear warheads, they committed suicide."

Her smile deepened.

"Per your orders, I informed the entire population of the dangers against your dynasty … and Mother Russia. All citizens have been advised to be on the lookout for sympathizers, and report them immediately. To the FSB."

"Then we will arrest, prosecute, and permanently remove them from our future."

"Not quite."

She glanced a quizzical look.

"We will … I suggest … retrieve a practice from the Gorbachev era."

"And what might that be?"

"Guilt by accusation."

"*Parfait.*" She paused. "That's *perfect* in French."

"You know how into French I am." He nodded at her bed.

"Well, prepare two Moscow Mules in memoriam to the Marxist ideologues. We'll quaff those. Then, get you naked. We'll celebrate."

She threw off her covers as an incentive.

CHAPTER 10

Living just at the West end of Big Bear Lake, it didn't take Micmac more than ten minutes to traverse the distance to Lenny and Alona's cabin in the upscale enclave known as Boulder Bay. He'd received the message that she wanted to talk. She let him in, and motioned him to a long, print covered sofa.

"Lenny actually wanted me to bring a case: Lipschitz v The State of New Hampshire."

Micmac shook his head. Lenny was like someone who'd stepped on his own foot, then stomped on the offending appendage to teach it a lesson. "I don't believe that New Hampshire has a black ops team, but, if they heard your husband's comments, they'd get one together and send it our way."

Alona nodded agreement.

"Is he allowed to speak freely on Social Media?"

"I've engaged parental controls. May have to beef that up."

"Wait! Like each of us, he possesses a CUR. You know. A CIA Universal Remote."

"The president ordered Jack to engage …"

"Parental controls. We're safe then."

Alona had a ready response that was interrupted.

"*Whine!*"

Lenny strutted in with his signature attitude. No matter how it manifested itself, it was always difficult to put a positive spin on it.

"Hi, Lenny," Micmac said. "We've been talking about you … and your New Hampshire visit not too long ago."

"Oh. The one where we were attacked by a large paramilitary force?"

"Actually, the force wasn't that big."

Micmac pre-empted a 'Lenny Launch' with "Take a seat, my diminutive friend. I've got video."

A non-plussed Lenny did as directed.

The former Navy SEAL and current spy-team member pulled from concealment his own CIA universal remote. He clicked in a special code.

The giant flat-screen across the room came to life. There were no advertisements or channel guides. They'd been stripped from the feed. A selected video replicating Lenny and Alona's vacation trip to Bretton Woods, as well as its famous nearby mountain, began.

It seemed like no matter the private time the team members took, they were always at risk for an attack by Illuminé affiliates. New Hampshire's Mount Washington proved to be no exception.

Lenny and Alona sat enraptured by precise lookalike figures doing exactly what they'd done at the time. Then, Lenny spotted an exception. "Hey, I reached out with my right hand, not my left!"

As if the video were alive, it corrected itself. The Lenny manifestation pulled in the errant arm, and extended the other.

"This Artificial Intelligence crap has got to go! See if you can square this away, Micmac, while we hide out in the bathroom."

As the two moved off, the gadget man heard Alona's situation-inspired plan.

"We can make love while we figure out what to do next."

CHAPTER 11

Hekka spent the entirety of her existence within the United States. Operations over the past three years had given her a real life understanding of other peoples across the globe, as well as how to survive when your life is in grave danger.

Magus Crayle observed her in deep thought. He wondered what his wife planned in further developing her research on her own tribe, the Serrano, and its possible linkage to tribes in Central Asia.

"What's next with respect to your research?"

"I kept it as a surprise. But … I'm off to Asia."

Her response drew a raised eyebrow. "This is my theory. Those who migrated here actually *indiginated* over in Central Asia."

"Let me save you some grief. When you finish and write your book, you'll get a professional editor. As did I for my spy novels. She won't let you make up words." A headshake later, he summed it up. "Indiginated."

She knew it was time. Hekka deployed her minimalist smile.

“Okay,” Crayle said. “I’ll listen, you talk.” He sat back with his 007 Martini.

“I’m headed overseas. For friendly territory. To visit our friend, Empress Ling, at her Hong Kong palace. I’ll fill her in on everything. We’ll go from there.”

“For one thing, you’ll be a long distance from the known migration path. It seems you’d want to backtrack from Eastern Siberia, where it once bridged to Alaska. Then, West all the way to Central Asia.”

“Correct. Phase 1. That’ll make the connection that’s fairly well accepted. Phase 2 is the new part. Connecting Central Asia to India.”

“Once you have that, the two routes established, the link between those Indians over there, and these Indians over here, will be complete. You’ll be finished.”

“Not quite. I’ll have to check out artifacts along the way. I’ll have to determine physical differences among the peoples, allowing for evolution and all over the thousands of years. And a few more items.”

“You might want to have ole Doc Rorschach along. He can do medical on your teams. Help with the physiology and other characteristics—the differences you expect to find. And, hey, he can do what he did for me on that Madeira Island. Before we took down Martim and his gang. In Portugal. He could embed a bunch of foreign languages in your brain. You’ll be able to communicate to folks in their native tongues.”

“I’ll take mind-messing by our favorite covert CIA doctor of research psychiatry under advisement. At least, that would keep him away from his prime subject. You.”

“About your trip. You know I support you one hundred per cent. I need to come along.”

“You’re forgetting. You’re President Stones’ new Director of Central Intelligence. You have a senate confirmation hearing coming up. All the while ensuring the world doesn’t explode. Remember?”

“Oh, yeah. That. I’ll go nuts cooped up at Langley. Perhaps I can get Kimbel to free me from my indenture.”

“Indenture?”

"People used to be taken as slaves in two modes. Chattel slavery meant someone owned you as property. Indentured slavery meant you had an obligation to fulfill, remaining a slave until that's done."

"I understand. I read a history paper on Africa. It said the slaves brought to the Western Hemisphere were indentured after a war in their homeland. The winners took the losers as indentured slaves, but took the opportunity to sell them to the Europeans, who brought them across the ocean."

"Boy, that must've been some community college you attended in San Bernardino."

Crayle referenced the eponymous Southern California county's capitol, bordering on the East side of the Los Angeles mega-county.

"Gotta start packing, Mag. Heading out tomorrow."

"Well, thanks for the heads up."

"Sorry about the short notice, but my publisher says now, and it's the one footing the bill."

"We have a one pound bag of perfect one-carat diamonds. That's more than enough to fund your journey."

"It's a relationship thing with publishers, I discovered. They want to feel some ownership."

"Talk about slavery. The amount they front to you probably becomes your indenture."

Hekka smirked. "It's not like that." And paused. "Not like that, I don't think."

"Alright. I'll dial up Kimbel and see if my senate hearing can be put off. If not, we'll stay in touch. Maybe Phoebe can tear away for a week or so. Go along. Keep you safe."

"A week? That's just in Hong Kong sharing Magus stories with Ling. Besides, I've got it covered."

"What ..."

Before another word could pass, the calm demeanor of the foregoing repartee headed due South.

"*Whine!*" echoed from the entryway.

CHAPTER 12

On her way to the so-called Sommers International Airport, Hekka intended to stop off at the CIA's covert Quarry Hospital to see Doc Rorschach and 'learn' languages. He claimed a new and improved methodology for installing knowledge in select covert operatives.

The trip East from the Fawnskin cabin seemed routine. But this time, her lover, husband, friend, and team leader had not joined her. She took in the beautiful landscape as she proceeded with care down the winding and precipitous Highway 18 to the valley floor. Then, after a left turn in to an operational rock quarry, into a special garage, and a trip 300 feet below ground on an express vehicle elevator, she walked with purpose into the familiar covert medical facility.

Doctor Permin Rorschach, one of the CIA's premier psychiatric researchers, appeared as always. A white lab coat hung on a moderate stature under a bald pate accentuated by a berm of white hair.

He remembered when he'd first met Magus Crayle's wife, Hekka Poppi. The stoic, half-blooded Serrano Indian rarely showed emotion.

If you told a half-decent joke, you'd receive her minimalist smile. If you could barely see her teeth, then the joke was hilarious.

Hekka took a seat. "Tell me, Doctor. Tell me about the memories. And your experimentation with Magus."

"Vee haff two possibilities." The doctor always reverted to his Swiss-accented English when he felt pressure. Because she'd admonished him not to tell Crayle of her visit, the accent engaged. Her calming presence, though, allowed him to recover quickly this time. "We purposely archived his memories and colluded in the Frenchman's attack on his Cobra on the highway North of Malibu. On the California Coast. Or he was the first subject in periodic archiving such as the computer center types routinely do."

"Which is the truth? Of the two possibilities?"

"He's a spy. I could tell him the truth, but then he'd haff to kill me."

Showing no response to his Swiss-accented joke, Hekka continued. "I need your assistance."

He now took serious interest. "You vant to be my subject?"

"I'm going on a research trip. I know you inserted conversational language knowledge of Portuguese during our last trip. Before we continued on to Portugal. It was in the town, Madeira. In the Azores."

"You should not know that. It was classified above Top Secret!"

"He tells me everything. And President Stones has conferred on both of us ultimate security clearance."

"I must check." He reached for his special sat phone.

Hekka intercepted his move with a serious grasp of the wrist. "Just asking would not go well for you."

The doctor glanced down at a quick motion by her hand. To the sheathed, ten-inch Bowie knife strapped to her waist.

He returned the phone to his desktop. "Vot do you vant?"

"Languages. I want languages. For my trip. It's far better to converse directly than to rely on translation. And multiple translators would pose a security threat, wouldn't they?" She handed him a paper she'd just plucked from her purse.

He studied it. “It will take some time to prepare.”

“Take as long as you need. You can download them to me via a secure satellite link. It will encrypt on your end, and decrypt on mine. What could go wrong?”

Rorschach started to launch into a long list of what could go wrong.

With a wave of her hand, Hekka cut him short. “That was rhetorical, as Magus would say.”

He quickly returned to listener mode.

“Oh. Obviously. I’ll need one of those head gear setups you used on Magus. To enable the data stream to embed it all into my brain. And, since I’m your new subject, how about a feature that recognizes the language being spoken by others? So I don’t have to ask.”

He smiled broadly. “More research. Take all the time I need.”

“Oh, did I say that? I’m sorry, Doctor Rorschach. I need it in a week.”

With that, she left the flummoxed covert doctor of psychiatric research in her wake as she disappeared.

CHAPTER 13

The day outside was unseasonably warm for early Winter. That's why as many who could in South Asia stayed inside with the air conditioning running at full song. Absent interruptions, it provided an environment perfect for serious thought.

Rustom Modi, the Mumbai-resident Parsi, came up with a strategy. He had a little help from Mag Crayle. Rusty, as his wife called him, would take full credit if it worked. If not, blame America. He considered taking things into his own hands to preserve secrecy, but he opted instead for the help of a proven genius. He would proceed in as straight forward a fashion as he could, overthrow the Iranian government, and reinstitute a Zoroastrian Persia.

Plan A represented his thwarted attempt to move the two bombs through southeastern Iran. As he had the Moscow-bound bomb for the czarina.

On to Plan B. After a great deal of research, he concluded he must take his effort North from Mumbai. With his wife, Leonor, stuck in Portugal for her father's funeral. Killed because of Crayle. He realized he needed to get busy in case she learned who was responsible, and took action. Perhaps destroying his dream. Rustom considered the situation in its entirety. He concluded that, best case, she'd be tied up in Sintra for months, settling her father's copious estate. He'd have the time needed to get things done in Iran.

He made his decision. He would sneak the mini-nukes in from the northeast. That's where the majority of Zoroastrians, who'd not fled the country's Islamic tyrants, resided. They would deliver the support he needed. Absolutely sure of that, Rustom Modi poured himself a drink and took a serious sip. It brought a broad smile. There was a helpful aspect unknown to the rest of the world. The Zoro underground railroad would move his small team and 'rugby' balls—to avoid detection—to within striking distance.

Of a sudden, he felt tremendously uncomfortable. He'd dreamt of this moment. It seemed like just a fantasy until he had acquired two mini-nuclear bombs, disguised as rugby balls. The potential to realize his dreams hit his nervous system like a ton of bricks. This wasn't what he was trained to do. He needed to make a call.

Rustom reached for the special phone. The one provided by Crayle.

Crayle picked up on the first ring.

The line connected, he initiated the handshake. "Lord, I was born a Ramblin' Man."

"Tryin' to make a livin' and doin' the best I can," on key, and melodically correct, completed the cycle.

Why his 'man-in-Washington' chose the opening lines of an Allman Brothers song, he didn't know. He'd remember to ask sometime. If he lived through this.

"Mr. Crayle, your offer has weighed heavily on me. I've thought, and I'm ready."

"You have a basic strategy? To overthrow the Iranian government? And replace it with a Persian one? Operated by those of Persian ancestry?"

"I must. The principles of the Persian faith, Zoroastrianism, must be returned to the people."

"There are quite a few Muslims, especially the ayatollahs and other clerics, who run—and dominate—Iran. Have you developed a spy service as I suggested?"

"Your suggestion sounded more like an order."

"Rest your heart, Rusty. I have zero interest in becoming the next King of Persia. Cyrus the Next, I'd be."

"Or Darius the Next."

Each could feel the smile on the other end.

"I have a plan, Mr. Crayle."

"Bring it, Rusty."

"We take the devices in the same manner I took the bomb that made its way to the Russian Czarina, Anastasia."

"The one that just about leveled Moscow, taking out Vladimir's Communist remnants, and turning his crypt and Lenin's tomb into molten dust vapor."

"Yes. And I've checked. The miniature nuclear device railroad I used before is still intact. We can transport the two bombs via the southeastern Iranian port. Bandar Beheshti. We'll use your own Blackstone Strategy. One bomb gets the leaders' to congregate, the other takes them out. Good so far?"

"That strategy has worked, but the ayatollahs might be wise to it from all the publicity. You can't afford to detonate half of your stockpile, and not get them to congregate."

"Our arrangement is made in Heaven. You can have your CIA test the waters for us. They can provide the real-time intelligence we need to perfectly time the second device's detonation."

"I noticed you said 'we' a lot with respect to inserting the nukes into Iran proper."

"When you were here in Mumbai at our first meet, you promised to assist."

"Strategist, yes. Operative, no," Crayle cautioned. "There is something happening on my end that you don't, and can't, know about. I will work with you to insure the highest probability of success possible. That you can count on."

Silence.

"Where will you place the new capitol, Rusty?"

"It has to be the ancient capitol of Persepolis. The people of the southwest Iranian region, Persis, from which Persia derived its name, ruled the Achaemenid Empire from 559 BC until 330 BC."

"I see. And I can feel the emotion in your voice. But it's time to get down the non-subjective aspects of this strategy. In utilizing the Systems Methodology Approach, we must identify Constraints—the things you can't do, and any limits on what you can do. Boundaries. Thresholds."

"Please explain, Mr. Crayle. In English terms I can understand."

"Such as blowing up the Strait of Hormuz. Or the Iranian oil fields."

"But those are such grand ideas."

Crayle had second thoughts.

"You must consider what you will have when you're done. You'll need the Straight and the fields for your economy. To pay the bills."

"But you will help by delivering all necessary American aid and assistance. It's what you promised right here in Mumbai not long ago."

"I've spoken to the president, and we're good on that. But you have to play nice here, Rusty. Leave the oil resources and pathways intact. Agreed?"

The Parsi had no alternative. "Agreed."

"So, let's each identify scenarios where bomb one gets them all together, plus the Quds and IRGC leaders. We'll determine the delivery aspect of bomb two at that point."

"Oh. About your wife."

"Hekka? Uh, she sends her regards."

"No. She's contacted my wife. To help her on her Indian migration project."

"Gotta go, Rusty. Talk soon."

He hung up the Rustom Modi-only phone, and dialed his wife on his official CIA Smartphone.

No answer. No ring.

He checked the display.

Comms dark.

"Crap!"

CHAPTER 14

When President Stones had the time and the need to meet with his CIA Director pro-tem, Jack Sommers, he'd jump into his specially-designed bathroom next to the Oval Office, drop down three hundred feet beneath the White House, and take the 300 mile per hour shuttle over to the remote STIF room under the Manassas Battlefield Park in Virginia. When it was Jack who received the summons to travel, he knew the president was either ultra busy or ultra pissed off. He made the journey to the under-D.C. STIF with that in mind.

He made the trip this time. His proximity pass got him inside the Sound and Technology Isolated Facility in short order.

The president was already waiting.

"I've got a slight problem, Jack."

"Hey. Problem Solvers R Us. Right here." He waved his hand for effect.

"We have a hearing coming up. A senate confirmation hearing. Those political piranhas are going to grill up and down anyone I send over. Since Mag has done off-the-books work in the past years, he'll have to stiff their giant egos full on. Any ideas?"

"It's easy. Don't send him over. Make up a bio. Send that."

"I'll ignore that. We'll have a fight getting Mag confirmed in the Senate. You know, to run the Agency. I received a call earlier. Susanna took it. Did the firewall thing. Anyway, there's an other-party senator who wants to know too much."

"We can't give up anything he's done because it's all off-the-books. Beyond classified. Why, Mr. President, I'm not sure you're even cleared at that level."

"Funny, Jack." Stones nodded to his right. "You see that fly over there? The fly on the wall? It doesn't require a clearance. No matter how high the level you and I need, it needs none."

Jack glanced in the indicated direction. "I don't see any fly."

"It's a stealth fly."

"Figurative, I believe, is the word, Mr. President."

"I've asked you many times to call me by my first name … Jack."

"Then it's Kimbel … Mr. President."

"Humor is not your strong suit. Keep the day job. If you can."

"Uh, what about this senator?"

"I'll keep you in the loop. Now, Mag only has this one thing left on his plate. The man in India. He calls himself a Parsi, right?"

"That's it. Should be able to wrap that up on the phone. Then, Mag's ready for that top spot at the Company. DCI."

"Details on the Parsi thing?"

"I could tell you … but …"

"But you don't know. You know, Jack, if your right hand wasn't so busy getting to know your private parts … in the biblical sense … you'd know what's going on."

"At least I don't do it in your presence. Of course, this is a STIF room …"

"Hmmm. This is serious, Jack. Mag's the one I need to revamp the CIA back to when it got things done. And kept itself secret."

Sommers nodded concurrence.

"Oh," Stones continued. "And that write up on the new CIA Mag promised. I haven't received anything. Do you have it?"

"Not yet."

"And where the hell is he? I grab my special Smartphone, and I get this dark cloud over the Mag comms icon."

He handed his phone over.

Jack reached out to take it.

"I'll have it checked out. Maybe a bug of some sort."

The president still gripped the phone. He pulled it back. "Actually, I do use it. Being president and leader of the free world. But you know that. So, where is he?"

"Uh, you're not going to like my answer."

"Jack, the U.S. Constitution forbids the government from resorting to torture to get answers to necessary questions. Such as mine. At least, I think it does. Do you recall?"

"It's been some time since I read the constitution, but I'm sure you're correct. Pretty sure."

"Pretty sure? So there might be some leeway?"

"No, Mr. President. No leeway. I remember that part."

"I'm not really into asking things twice ..."

"Wait! Oh! I've got it!"

"You have the document I require? The remake of the CIA document?"

"No! Not that! I've got how you can get Mag past the Senate Intel Committee!"

"This better be good. I believe I still have access via the new French head of state to his dad's medieval torture devices."

For the first time in the meeting, Jack Sommers relaxed just a bit. "Yeah, Kimbel. This is *that* good."

CHAPTER 15

Magus Crayle, the Director of Central Intelligence to be, knew he was getting himself in deep. Real deep.

He promised the president, his friend, something he hadn't yet delivered. While he had prepared the document en route, he needed to share it in person in the STIF with Kimbel. Hard to do when your next stop in the team's Falcon 9X was Mumbai, India.

"Wheels down in fifteen," came over the announcing system. "Buckle up!"

Crayle reckoned Marli and Flori, who shared piloting duties for the off-the-books Strategic Solutions Office ops team, apparently had the same pilot training. Always "*Wheels up—buckle up*, then *wheels down*. All it needed was *buckle down* to make it symmetric.

The landing at the international airport was the usual text book outcome. They taxied to a stop just seconds before Crayle observed Rustom Modi motor up and park his Mercedes near the jet's front hatch.

Down and out with luggage in hand, he shocked his most recent colleague in geopolitical disruption with his disguise. Someone who knew of such things would've taken him for a long-haired hippie freak from the 1960s.

The drive out to the airport had worn Modi out. An hour to travel the handful of miles. Normally, a paid driver would have suffered the indignities of getting to Mumbai International, but a special guest, not to be noticed, was the target. The Parsi came alone.

His faux reason for vehicular access to the private terminal was a done deal. No worries there.

As he'd pulled up to the parked plane, a man he did not recognize approached.

Full beard and shoulder length hair. Still, the 6'3" frame kept him in the ballpark.

"I thought you weren't wanting to be noticed," the slightly shorter man said in a critical tone. He then broke into a smile, extending his hand.

Crayle took it, but did not squeeze as customary in the West.

He introduced Micmac, who sported his interpretation of a blonde guitar god hairdo, and who'd trailed behind.

Rustom Modi led the pair to their ride. He shared a bit during the first mile, but took note of his travel-weary guests and their inability to engage. The remainder of the return back through the uber vibrant city of Mumbai waxed silent, though each had plenty to say.

Back inside Rusty's villa in the upscale Malabar Hill neighborhood, they took a moment to unwind. And reflect.

"Thank you for coming. I'd love to hear your excuse for getting away from Washington, but another time. Nice of your president to give you sufficient leave."

Crayle didn't point out that he'd just disappeared off the grid. He'd followed the old adage, "It's easier to ask forgiveness, sometimes, than to ask permission." He hoped Kimbel Stones would agree.

"I know you like our Kingfisher Beer. I ordered in a couple of cases."

"What we have planned is sobering enough. How, Rusty, are we getting your pair of nukes, disguised as rugby balls, into Iran?"

• • •

Rusty surprised Crayle. He wasn't ready to chat, he was ready to go. In short order they arrived at their operational transportation. Then, loaded up, and away.

The rickety old bus, after hours of bumpy travel and a couple of stops for potty, petrol, and McDonalds veggie burgers, finally rolled into yet another town.

As they entered, Crayle saw the magnificent sight of a temple. Resplendent white all over, it sported numerous domes, perhaps twenty on top, and in this moment brought forth the peace engendered in the Hindu religion. All of the world's good people deserved peace. This sight just reaffirmed his long-held belief.

The driver pulled the ancient vehicle into a parking lot and managed to grab the last two spots. The hoots and yells from drivers behind were not verbal manifestations of applause. It seemed that early in India's Winter, lots of folks from the mountainous North found refuge in this, the province known as Gujarat.

"Okay," Rustom said. "This town is called Bhuj. Not far North of where the western Indian coast meets the Arabian Sea. We'll spend the night at this, the Regenta Resort and enjoy some delicious curry for dinner. At their Gazebo Open Air Restaurant."

Crayle couldn't resist. "I saw another place just a couple of blocks down. The 2 Amigos."

"You might feel more comfortable with Mexican food, being from Southern California, Mr. Crayle, but curry and other Indian specialties will help you acclimate to the environment in which we shall operate."

"Darn. I was looking forward to a couple of tandoori tacos."

Rustom didn't get rich by not being smart, and quick. "You are familiar with this restaurant?"

Micmac couldn't resist. "Even Lenny would've laughed at that one, Rusty."

The man up front was back in charge. "We'll catch some real sleep. Tomorrow, our operation begins in earnest."

Crayle barely heard the Parsi's pronouncement. He stared out the window. And wondered. What in the world was he doing? He'd made a ridiculous promise to a man in India who identified as a Persian. In their prior meeting, said man had kidnapped he and his wife, Hekka, and had them brought to him. In the next instant, he had the answer. It just didn't compute. He'd seen the good that could come from a remade and inherently peaceful Iran. No more terrorism, just peace. After all, wasn't that what the Zoroastrian religion prescribed? And with peace instilled, prosperity for everyone would be all but guaranteed. Wouldn't it?

"Mr. Crayle," came at him from the front. "We're getting off now."

His busted reverie took a back seat to the here and now.

He followed Micmac off the bus.

• • •

The dinner curry was hot. Micmac compared it to a Marshall amplifier turned up to eleven. Maybe even a twelve.

After what passed for Alka-Seltzer in quantity, the American spies slid into their beds. And slept.

CHAPTER 16

Oblivious to what was going on in India or anywhere else, Hekka attempted to rest on the trans-Pacific flight. The Crayle team's Dassault Falcon jet carried her toward the beginning of the long trek across Central Asia that lay ahead. Of her two cohorts, Phoebe had nestled into the bed and slept the whole way.

Hekka, at first, thanked the gods that Lenny had decided to take her own husband's lead. He'd write a novel. He swore he'd stay out of the spy arena, worried he might wrongly give away a source or a method or two. That should keep him busy and out of mischief, she thought. However, it was annoying as he played the parts and dialogs out loud. She stepped into the flight deck and shut the door to the main cabin. Jack Sommers' ex-wife, Marli, replete with her bright red lipstick and outsized Hollywood sunglasses, kept her company and flew the jet as well. Something about walking and chewing gum.

They landed at Hong Kong's Chek Lap Kok airport as they'd done several times before. A light rain accompanied them on their royal limo ride to the palace of the very young, but wise beyond her years, Empress Ling.

Courtiers met them with Chin-period reproduction umbrellas. The fifty foot trek to and through the large, heavy doors got them just a bit wet.

Things brightened up as soon as they arrived inside. It wasn't just the ornate beauty of the royal palace fabricated by Ling's husband atop Victoria Peak a short couple of years before. More so, it was their hostess.

Ling was there with her trademark rounded lips smile and warm greeting. They moved quickly into the reception chamber. A doffing of plastic rainwear later, and her guests were ready for some hot tea, which Yellow Daughter had prepared.

"Welcome, Hekka. Welcome, Phoebe. And Mr. Lipschitz. Please ..." She waved at a $25,000 period replica sofa, and the tea service.

"It is so good to see you."

"And you, Ling. I'm on my quest no matter what, but your help at the outset and paving my way at least to the western boundary of China is so welcomed."

"Especially since you always carry weapons. We should discuss how you will be covered when you depart my realm."

Unable to remain in the background as his trip role of bodyguard required, Lenny broke in.

"I remember you've got a state-of-the-art video game room. You two can chat while I play. How's that for altruism?"

"No, that sounds good," Phoebe injected. "I like the games where you shoot the bad guys." She glanced over at her diminutive and typically offensive colleague. "Like with a .45 caliber Glock 30." She reached behind, patting the compact lump covered by her blouse.

Ling produced an understanding nod, and considered the possibilities. "Yellow will show you to the room. Remember, though. You don't have much time here. Perhaps an hour. Your schedule through Central Asia is, I've been informed, quite rigorous."

Off they went, trailing Yellow Daughter, Lenny whining about something until out of earshot.

Ling and Hekka went for the teacups.

"Lenny can be a pill sometimes," Hekka observed.

"He's been here before." The empress' comment brought the signature minimalist smile in return.

"Enough said on that account. Please, give me a snapshot of what's to come."

"You'll fly from here to the Xinjiang capitol. It's a long flight. Perhaps you could stow your Mr. Lipschitz with the luggage. There are no animals being transported, so you wouldn't have to worry about them biting him."

"Or he, them."

It was funny. Each time in conversation with Ling, she felt as if she were with a sister. She'd never had one. Two brothers. Heavy duty paratroopers both.

"You'll land just northeast of the center of the Semi-Autonomous Region. Your first and permanent guide will fill you in on details, and show you things of the past. Then, out to the wild West, and a second guide will join you. She knows that area and its peoples, past and present, very well. Both women are young, but very special."

Their wonderful and productive repartee was interrupted.

Lenny.

As the two bodyguards strode back into the room.

"She cheated!"

Phoebe's countenance gave away who won, too.

Ling responded to the sudden ringing of a bell.

"Ah, time to go. Good luck, Hekka. And to you as well, Phoebe and Mr. Lipschitz."

"It's Lenny," he remarked.

"Yes. Lenny."

"Whine."

They all produced a courtesy bow, and Yellow led them out to the Empress' limo for an uneventful trip back to the Lantau Island airport. Hong Kong International.

CHAPTER 17

As she headed outside to the limo, Hekka extracted her Smartphone. She'd give aforementioned husband a call. But stopped short. He'd take in where she was and what she was doing, and in minutes, perhaps seconds, comprehend her quest's primary components, the specialized nature of each, their interrelationships, and then the relationship of the whole to what he termed its environment. To a standard person, that could take days or months. To a genius like him, it was intuitive. While his breakdown and analysis of everything could help her enormously, she needed to do this one—this quest—on her own. Somewhere along the journey, she would give him a call. Perform a sitrep. Oh, there. She was thinking like him.

• • •

Back on the jet, Hekka Crayle departed Hong Kong's Chek Lap Kok international airport with a mindful of potential regrets. In parting, Ling had informed her that someone would meet her upon arrival in Ürümqi. The person would serve as the guide for her trip along the ancient Silk Road. Her trip West. At least, that was the original plan. On second thoughts, given Hekka's unfamiliarity with Xinjiang, its language, and customs, the Empress-supplied guide had been spirited to Hong Kong and now sat across from her.

It remained in Hekka's mind how easily Ling used Magus' given name versus Mr. Crayle. She just knew there was more to know about their past relationship. The question? Did she really want that knowledge? Curiosity, she recalled, did not do well for the cat.

And Ling had actually said, "I'm sorry for all the familiar references to your husband. I was just one of the twelve Chin Yao-wu adopted daughters. He assigned us each a color. And provided a cheongsam dress in that color. As you know, I was Black Daughter. And because of father's past, he never touched us … in that way. But, for the two years your husband was here, we were cordial, but that's all. I mean that. We were cordial."

She'd taken a minute. Then, responded with, "It's okay, Ling. I know you've had, continued to have, and shall continue to maintain a personal, cordial and platonic link to him."

Unusual for an empress, Ling had stepped closer. She'd given a hug.

Hekka responded with, "If something ever happens to me, you two might …"

"Please," the empress cut her short. "Your jet awaits."

CHAPTER 18

The next morning in westernmost India, the operational team, all showered and dressed, remounted the bus and headed South. After what Crayle estimated at about fifty miles and perhaps one relentless hour of jostling this way and that, they finally drove over a crest, and a wondrous sight came into view.

"That, my friends," Rustom informed them, "is the Arabian Sea. In all, or at least some, of its splendor. You passed by before, Mr. Crayle, when your cruise ship sailed from Muscat, Oman to Mumbai. When we first met."

The 'meeting' had been more of a kidnapping, but a little time had healed the wound. They'd found a major common interest.

The road continued downhill to a quaint appearing fishing village. A sign, including English translations, declared it as Rapur.

The American spy and presidential confidant examined the landscape. "It doesn't look from here to be a hotbed of international smuggling."

"These items we carry appear to be rugby balls, Mr. Crayle. No indication whatsoever that miniaturized nuclear warheads reside inside."

"Point taken, Rusty."

The bus slowed after several near traffic mishaps, stopping at a pier.

"It's the white boat. Near the end. The two men and their teenage sons smuggle all the time. Probably enough to someday retire in New Jersey."

Rustom tried to deadpan, but a smile broke through.

He led his entourage down the dock way to the boat.

The two boys had achieved a quite good English language speaking ability, but couldn't pass up a chance to show off their mimicking of Number 5 in the movie, Short Circuit.

But things were about to get serious. Their father reeled them in.

Rustom introduced everyone. Then, he smiled naturally at the boy's antics.

Crayle's thoughts regained focus on what came next.

His small team, and the boat crew, were about to transport two nuclear devices into a hostile foreign country, and detonate them to affect a regime change. To modify that country forever, its impact on the Middle East, and the world. Crayle shook his head. Life could be insane at times.

"We have gifts for the regime." Rustom hoisted one of the mini-nukes.

"Oh," said the boat owner and de facto captain. "A rugby ball. Just like the last time. I shall look for the same Iranian guards—they hang out in groups—to get you past with minimum delay, and baksheesh."

"Thank you. Keeping the bribes down will be most helpful."

He placed the 'rugby ball' back in the duffel with its mate, then handed it over. With that, all but one of the Modi team carefully transitioned to the watercraft. Micmac, stationed next to the tie-down cleats, prepared to cast off and hop in.

One of the sons hopped up onto the pier, casting him a look.

“Must be his job,” the former SEAL observed. “Probably union.”

The young man loosened the tether, tossed it into the boat, and the two followed it in.

The associate of the man-in-charge cranked the engine. The craft and its inhabitants sped out into the Arabian Sea.

The captain put the morning sun behind them as he turned West, then cranked the motor to flank speed.

Before thirty minutes could elapse, the team members relaxed themselves to their normal heart rates. It was only when the captain suddenly turned North that those rates ramped back up.

The two Americans still wore sunglasses. So the not-so-casual observer couldn’t tell where they were looking. Or what caught their interest. Or their focus. Facing a bit away from their target could throw off an onlooker.

Crayle caught facial movement from his colleague. Micmac pursed his lips, and pushed them to one side. Only one person they both knew possessed that affectation. Lenny’s wife, Alona. It unintentionally signaled that she wasn’t buying whatever a speaker was selling. The defense attorney in her needed to probe deeper to the core. She’d gained notoriety by seeing through her own client’s words to the masqueraded reality. In a landmark move, and using her findings, she then proved, beyond a shadow of a doubt, her client’s guilt.

Alona wasn’t the only winner. Justice won.

Crayle picked up on it. His cohort used non-verbal means to communicate the need to penetrate Rustom Modi’s strong exterior defenses. Their lives depended on it. Without turning his head toward him, he mirrored his former SEAL team member’s signal in what Micmac would call an ACK. An acknowledgement.

They weren’t the only ones subject to anomalies.

Rustom yelled over the din. “Where are you taking us, Captain!”

“Be at ease, my brother. We must pick up some goods, illegal in Iran, to deliver. Drugs, sex slaves. Otherwise, the border guards might become suspicious. I’ve heard the Iranian jails are brutal.”

CHAPTER 19

They sailed North until the captain announced, "We cross now into Pakistani waters. Amongst the fishing vessels, it should be no problem."

Rustom didn't know about any interim stops. Especially in Pakistan. It could be necessary to intervene. Now was the time to know.

"You're not picking up contraband in the capitol, I hope. We're trying not to be noticed. In Karachi, they notice everything."

"No, no," the man laughed. "Offshore of the Mouths of the Indus, a … uh … fishing boat will bring the contraband. It is good that you are so aware. Our sons pick up good ideas from our wise customers. Like yourselves."

Crayle wondered how many clients the captain had that were spies. With nuclear capability.

• • •

Hours later, and with six crates that must've held drugs, and four so-called sex slaves—in reality, Pakistani spies—the full boat crossed into Iranian waters just a few klicks from their destination. The port town of Bandar Beheshti.

No sooner did they pull up to the dock, then all hell broke loose.

Lights!

Sirens!

Patrol boats!

Police cars!

All heading their way

Crayle's head spun to the sex slaves.

Just in time to see them dive over the side into the water. And swim beneath the pier.

Five police units screeched to a stop on the pier next to them.

In short order, the coast guard boats pulled up outboard of them.

Confusion appeared to have been major course work at the Iranian police academy, if there was one.

Finally, the ranking officer approached the boat captain. He asked where were the women spies his intel alert had indicated.

Like others who survived in his inherently dangerous business, the captain was verbally quick on his feet. In passable Farsi, he explained that he knew of no such spies. He waved his hand from stem to stern of the boat, and shrugged.

The officer got the drift. No females. No female spies. But he needed blood. He ordered the patrol boats to escort this guilty-of-something bunch out to sea, and out of Iranian territory. Right after his men removed the contraband boxes of drugs. They placed them in the trunk of a private vehicle nearby, which belonged to the border guard chief. For later inspection. And disposition. Actually, the officer's older brother's car.

After a quick stop at a nearby fueling station, the boat was escorted 'off premises' to the Pakistani border. The patrol boat officer let them off with a dire warning. Never come this way again … if they had Pakistani spies aboard. Especially those disguised as sex slaves.

"I'm so sorry," the captain told him as he continued their journey to the southeast.

Magus Crayle and Rustom Modi glared at the captain.
A major operation scrubbed due to a failed infil.
Clearly, someone needed to be held to account.
They knew just what to do.
Rock—Paper—Scissors!

CHAPTER 20

The situation in the White House wasn't improving. And it wasn't in the Situation Room. Rather, it was deep below ground in the very special sound and technology isolated facility, STIF, with the consternation and appeasement delivered by the U.S. president and covert advisor, respectively. President Kimbel Stones called for the meet, and initiated the confab.

Jack Sommers filled in all the blanks he could. He brought out the covert recordings for the ultimate in veracity, and initiated them on the STIF's flat screen.

Immediately, Stones recognized the players.

• • •

The Queen of Sweden stood and, unlike her husband, was able to continue the conversation while replacing her underwear.

"You're King of France, Jean-Marc. Lord of all that is France. But your paranoia prevents you from leaving the palace. You should see someone. A specialist."

The man of her attentions was now fully dressed.

"And how can I be sure the specialist won't kill me? Look, all the political types and their power were displaced when the French government leaders were wiped out during their trip in China. The remnants want me dead. I'm sure of it."

"It's easy. Do what Russia's new czarina did. She got her enemies in one place, the Moscow Red Square, and then blew them up. She employed the Magus Crayle Blackstone Strategy. You know that."

"As usual, you are right. With the unceasing turmoil in the Middle East, along with the recent regime change in China, I need to meet with him again. But right here at Versailles."

"I'll get right on that, Your Excellency. But first …"

She began to remove her pair of garments. "How quickly I forget what your excellence is like."

"It's been less than five minutes."

She hopped back onto the bed.

"And …"

• • •

"And here's Russia," Jack announced. He pressed on the Universal Remote.

Czarina Anastasia Romanova appeared genuinely upset. Yes, she lived in Russia's number one city, Saint Petersburg. Yes, she resided in one of the most sumptuous palace dwellings on the planet—the former palace of Catherine the Great. Where was her chief advisor? Aside from Raspi, where was everyone else? She had enough lovers in her household that they could unionize. Then, what?

A familiar voice entered the room.

"Not to worry whatever worries your pretty head. I have good news. From Iran."

"Come to bed. You can whisper it in my ear."

As activities began, Raspi provided the sitrep regarding the czarina's greatest concern.

"There's turmoil inside Iran's leadership. They need to keep supporting their terrorist surrogates throughout the Middle East, and somehow accede to promises made, under extreme duress, to the American president. His representative, Mr. Crayle, holds damning evidence over their heads. World Peace, he wants."

"That's extortion," she moaned.

"Yes. And it works well for us. The Iranians are asking for guidance."

The whispered commentaries ended abruptly.

Jack smiled at the depth and accuracy of the intel.

• • •

"Here's China."

The president watched, enraptured.

Comfortable in her Hong Kong palace, Empress Ling grew impatient easily. Partly because of her early twenties youth, and the rest because she was Empress Of All China. She pulled a nearby lanyard to summon her number one.

Yellow Daughter was through the tall, elaborate, and beautiful floor-to-ceiling drapes and across the room in seconds.

She smiled. "Yes, Your Highness."

"Enough of that, Yellow. Why have I not heard that my ground breaking pronouncements have been delivered by Mrs. Crayle in Xinjiang?"

"I'm keeping contact with the Uighur operative. We are coordinating the timing of the speech with the necessities of Mrs. Crayle's research trip. Expect it soon. I'll let you know right away."

"Yes. Do that. The very minute you know. And record it. I want to hear every word."

• • •

Back to the STIF.

Stones and Sommers let the intel seep in. The intelligence communities didn't just collect data points to put in a data base, they stood back and attempted to grasp the feel of it. Especially as it might evolve over the next year. Or two. Or three. The talent to foresee future trends, especially in the global sense, was not innate. It developed over time and experiences. Except, of course, for players like the absent Crayle, for whom it was intuitive.

"The situation in the Middle East isn't getting any better, Jack. Surely, the passage of time hasn't helped."

"You've got the modern day remnants of tribes. With artificial lines drawn around groups of them, and called borders."

"It's an excessively complex situation. Iran is run by a group of religious leaders, who claim totalitarian authority from the Creator Himself."

"The type of people who thrive on total power over others are all the same. And the over-claiming of religious authority? You take what they actually do, and then conclude they've chosen a pathway directly to Eternal Hell. When their time here is done."

"Yeah. It's as if they commit some atrocity, then figure they're doomed to Hell anyway, and have nothing really to lose. It's hard getting worse punishment than Hell for Eternity."

"Yes, but in their Middle East religion, they believe in gradations of Hell. So it can get worse."

Stones appeared maximum perplexed. "I need Magus. He can figure this out. Have you heard anything?"

"Not even an encrypted peep. I'll let you know ASAP when I do. We'll put him to work on this Middle East debacle."

The president released a deep sigh. "Yes, Jack. I just hope he's okay."

CHAPTER 21

"Yoo-hoo!"

The intercom voice jarred those in the main cabin and bedroom out of their sleep.

"Out of HKG, Hong Kong International. Fueled up in CTU. Chengdu, China. Next stop, URC. Diwopu International. Ürümqi, Xinjiang, China. Nine hours total when we're down. Not bad."

The groans and moans didn't make it into the flight deck.

"Landing in thirty," came pilot Marli Sommers voice once more over the sound system. "Buckle up ..." And then, as though a countdown had taken place. "Now!"

Hekka imagined the laugh after Marli clicked off. With that bright red lipstick and Hollywood sunglasses as an underscore.

"C'mon, Arzu. Let's get legal."

The tan young woman, a model's statuesque 5'9" with bottle-sourced strawberry blonde hair, followed her employer's lead.

Buckled and cinched, they awaited the feather light touch down characteristic of the plane and the pilot.

"As you know, Ürümqi suffered devastation from an atomic blast just a couple of years ago. We Uighurs, regardless of ethnic background, will jump to a task like rebuilding."

"Tell me."

"The initial work involved saving those who could be saved. When rescue became recovery, we rebuilt the airport. We received surprising good assistance from the Han Chinese."

"They needed to get their soldiers … and their spies … in and out."

"Just so."

"So the airport ahead is ready for us. Rebuilt?"

"From scratch, as you'd say. It is modern with no pot holes or uneven breaks in the tarmac."

"So we'll avoid Mr. Toad's Wild Ride when we come in."

"I'm sorry?"

"What did you do before you became a tour guide, Arzu?"

"Oh. I served in the Navy."

"Xinjiang had a Navy? You're as landlocked as any nation on Earth."

"The Chinese Navy. I travelled a lot, and learned a lot. And you're right. Ürümqi is the furthest city from an ocean in the world. 2250 kilometers. 1395 miles."

"Where'd you go?"

"Africa. India. Everywhere the Hans have inserted themselves. They were still focused on that Communist ideal of world domination. Oh. Hong Kong, too."

"Hong Kong? Hmmm."

"We sailed out of Shanghai. It was on liberty in Hong Kong that I first met Empress Ling. She wasn't an empress yet. And her adoptive father, Chin Yao-wu, had not yet overthrown the Hans."

"Oh? So her hooking you up with me as a tour guide has some backstory." Raised eyebrows. Like the spy game Hekka played on a daily basis, surprises seemed to infiltrate normal life. "Interesting. Tell me how you met."

"I ended up at the Hard Rock Café near downtown. Ling and her sisters were all there for the rock music. We like that music here in Xinjiang."

"Well, Phoebe's husband is a rock musician. Perhaps we can set up a tour stop," Hekka kidded.

"I would help! That would be great! I think we can be friends. My friends call me Arzie."

"Arzu. I'm keeping my eye on the ball here. I've come to conduct serious research regarding the migrations that led my people from your part of the world to North America."

The Uighur remained excited by the prospect of a new friend. Especially one so interesting. And an American, too. "Ling informed me of your mission. And I've secured intel—" Oops.

Hekka's eyes bored into Arzu's.

"Intel?"

A few heavy near threats passed unspoken. "You're not just a tour guide. Are you?"

"I ... I'm not formally trained. Like my Uighur comrades. The Hans from the Ministry of State Security get comprehensive training. We read books."

"James Bond?"

"All of them. I have a confession."

"Yes?"

"Ling recently started me on the books written by your husband."

"You've read *The Water Diamonds*?"

Hekka remembered the book quite well. And that her husband had actually created Book 2, *The Blackstone Strategy*, from a for-real CIA mission to benefit the late Emperor of China, Chin Yao-wu.

She moved on.

"Yes. His publicist uses the 'ripped from the headlines' approach to marketing."

Arzu became saddened by her thoughts. "The Blackstone story lays out the nuclear attack on Ürümqi. That killed so many, and devastated others. All so the Han Communist leaders would be forced to congregate in Beijing to deal with a perceived, nuclear-armed, Muslim extremist threat that had allowed a weapon in their possession to pre-detonate. How your husband put all that together from publicized events has me believe that your husband is very smart."

"He's that, all right."

"After that, a second bomb in the Beijing Underground City killed most of the assembled leaders, and toppled the Communist regime."

"Yes, and Chin Yao-wu stepped into the void and used the forged ancient jade stone inscription to secure a renewed Chin empire with himself on top."

"I'm reading *The Crystal Seduction*—your husband's third—to learn about the special jade stone. You must congratulate Mr. Crayle for me. His novels are like history told in fictional format."

Hekka didn't point out that his books were not overloaded with actual fiction.

"Down in five," Marli proclaimed over the intercom.

The touch down went as smooth as glass. The post-bomb construction and upgrades at the airport yielded a first class surface for the team's Falcon business jet to alight and roll smoothly to its terminal resting place.

CHAPTER 22

They deplaned, latched onto their suitcases, and trekked a short fifty steps to their awaiting vehicle. The supersized Hummer with oversized knobby tires implied their destination involved some serious off-road work. Fine, Hekka considered. She needed to go wherever the artifacts were. It seemed Ling and Arzu were covering all bases. Still, staying unnoticed in a contraption that looked like it belonged in a stadium would present a challenge.

Arzu jumped in behind the wheel, motioning Hekka to take shotgun. Lenny could share the back seat with Phoebe.

"Since you're brand new here, I'll give you, as we Uighurs say, the lay of the land." She produced a bit of a smile.

"Ürümqi is the capitol of Xinjiang Semi-Autonomous Region. As you will see from the sky scrapers, and the heavy smog, it is the commercial center for this part of China's territories. There ahead in the distance is the Central Business District with its skyscrapers. I believe you have those, too."

She waited.

Silence.

"Ah. Good listeners. I like that. We'll be heading out this airport access road to the expressway. Then on to our next destination. But first, we'll stop for lunch. Lenny? How about you make the choice?"

"Alright."

"There's a spot called The Aroma Restaurant. How about that one?"

"I bet the food stinks." Lenny laughed.

"Perhaps the next one is more suitable. Pizza and beer. Fish and chips. It's called FUBAR."

Lenny roared. Phoebe shook her head.

Hekka leaned over close to the Uighur, and expanded the acronym.

"Oh. Don't want to go there. Tell you what we'll do. We'll stop off the highway at the Texas Café. Steaks and burritos. How's that?"

"Fine," was the conclusive and muted response.

There was something in the furthest reaches of Hekka's mind. She seemed to remember a Texas Restaurant. In Hong Kong. Across from the Monday Club. Oh, well.

"All that greenery dead ahead is the People's Park. It's great for a stroll. You can pause for a few moments at Mirror Lake. It's good for reflecting."

She didn't have to wait. Lenny thought that one was funny.

Arzu pulled them off the highway and into the Texas Café parking lot. In short order, the hostess seated them in a large, cushy booth. Their guide resumed, passing on the interesting points of Xinjiang's capitol city.

"There are various populations in the capitol city. Various languages, customs, and attitudes."

"That's fine, but how do we dial 911 if any of those attitudes gets out of hand?"

"Not to worry. The population is highly controlled. Perhaps not so much outside the capitol."

"China keeps a tight leash, I've heard."

"That was the case with the Communists. In Beijing. When Emperor Chin overthrew them and took over, he was too busy to change things. Better for him to focus on consolidating power. That was he word he used. Consolidating."

"And what now? With him gone, and Empress Ling in the top seat?"

"The people of China took to her immediately. She'll probably be too busy as well, especially for someone so young, to concern herself with China's far West, and largest province."

"What about the capitol itself?"

"It has a population of a few million. I'll get the latest figure off the Internet when I have a spare moment. Anyway, the capitol's positioned in a break in the East-West mountain string that divides the province North and South. With deserts on both side. As for Indian migrations, we'll see what we can find. You know, for your quest."

"I want to thank you ahead for what we might find. It's like the world's greatest treasure hunt."

"Many, many, many have come to our land, and taken away to Europe or other places, or destroyed, our historical artifacts. But many still remain. I've researched heavily. You trip is engineered, if I may say that, for your benefit."

"Then let's get going. It seems we have a lot of work ahead."

They trouped to the Hummer on steroids, and were off.

CHAPTER 23

On a tight schedule, the grand tour would wait. Still, Hekka, Phoebe, and Lenny took in the sights as they passed by. Perhaps some day, they'd come back. And spend some time.

Arzu had the Hummer headed out of the Xinjiang capitol on the Hetan Expressway. Southward, it followed on the West side of the Ürümqi River. At six lanes, it was impressive for this part of the world.

"Listen to what I say. It will help you here in Ürümqi, and throughout Xinjiang. First, the basic information."

Seated in the back seat to the right of Phoebe, Lenny leaned his head against the window.

"Ürümqi is our capitol city. And our center of culture and commerce. It has 3.5 million people. And it continues to grow. It is most important in the Chinese economy."

Lenny began to snore.

The Uighur retained her composure, and sense of humor. "Phoebe? If you would just lean right across your friend, and loosen the door latch, I'll watch for a sharp left turn up ahead."

Phoebe caught herself considering the notion. Except she and Lenny constituted the protection detail with Hekka responsibility. She did lean right, but only so Arzu could see her smile in the rearview mirror. It only took her a few minutes to, like Lenny, drop off.

"The Chinese call our land the Xinjiang Uighur Semi-Autonomous Zone. They moved so many Han Chinese here, our city is seventy-five percent them. We have a special presence of the MSS. Ministry of State Security. Spies." She gave a moment for that to be digested. "Our status designation as Autonomous is Orwellian."

"You studied George Orwell?" asked her only awake passenger.

"I did. I learned the term, diametric opposite."

"I'm impressed."

"We have an excellent school here. Xinjiang University. Top notch academics. Perhaps you will someday return as visiting Professor Crayle."

Hekka thought of her husband. With quite enough mathematics and systems methodology for his own PhD. And professorship. Hmmm … a life after the CIA.

Arzu continued slowly in the heavy traffic, headed South. That the streets were teeming with business people posed no surprise. Skyscrapers that announced the presence of a central business district loomed not far away.

"By the way, the temperatures today are typical for this time of year. My weather app indicated we should expect a twenty-four degrees Fahrenheit high and a nine degree Fahrenheit low tonight. Only half an inch of precipitation falls on average this month. Oh, and time wise, Beijing forced China into a single time zone. Our sun comes up at 9:45 AM."

Hekka noted that she felt a bit warm in her thermal underwear, sweater, and parka on top of the heater running at full blast.

Arzu continued her monolog.

"Our town is the regional center for rail, road, and air traffic. A transportation hub. Unfortunately, industrial and dust smog puts us in the top ten cities for worst pollution. It may surprise you that

China has seven of those top ten. A real problem. We wear masks not to prevent disease spread, but in order to breathe."

"What about the surrounding area that my people may have crossed thousands of years ago?"

"Yes. To the North lies the Junggar Basin. To the South, the Tarim Basin. Splitting them, the Tien Shan mountains to your right. In fact, those mountains split Xinjiang, North from South. To your left, East, are the Bogda Shan, with Bogda Peak over 17,000 feet above sea level. And there's a beautiful body of water near it. Heaven Lake is the English. Too far to visit on this trip."

Hekka already knew that *Shan* meant mountains. Part of Doctor Rorschach's mental implants ordered up before she left on her trip. Spies needed to know a lot, she reasoned, but not let others know you knew. Her's was no profession for anyone with an ego.

"Speaking of your husband's novels, this city began as Dihua. Lots of spies and intrigues, say the historians. That nature continues on still today." Arzu cast a quick smile Hekka's way.

Yes, Hekka thought. More than you know. But this won't be a spy trip. Just three spies gathering intel. About people thousands of years ago.

"By the way, Hekka. Ürümqi means beautiful pastures in Mongolian. The Kazakhs were itinerant. The families would graze livestock not far from here. They would build round, flat-topped living quarters called yurts. Like the Mongols."

"That interests me. My ancestors in Southern California did something similar." She pulled up a picture on her Smartphone. "This one is called the Serrano Big House. It's on our Morongo Reservation."

Arzu took a quick glance. Interrupted by an epiphany.

"Oh, I almost forgot. There were well-preserved mummies found here indicating that Persians from northeastern Iran made it this far. Perhaps we can check them out for facial similarities."

CHAPTER 24

They'd survived. Barely. When Crayle's eyes popped open, he was peering into the darkness. With no idea how long he'd been out.

A bump. A big one. He quickly determined his mode of transportation. Long gone was the watercraft that had carried them to the Iranian port, and back.

Translucent shades were drawn throughout the bus, including the windshield. Sure. No one could see in. No facial recognition. But having the driver see where he was going in the dark seemed to be a good idea. Crayle needed to have a brief chat with Rustom about tradecraft overreach.

In that instant, the Earth must've slipped a gear. The sun verily poured in from their right, the East, as if someone had flipped a multi-bladed, industrial duty switch.

The shades cut the glare in half. Just enough.

Rustom said something to the driver. Since the bus was headed North, he could free up the windscreen, and actually see where they were going. Stay on the road, in other words.

With the shades in front of the driver stowed, Crayle saw what lay ahead. And was amazed.

The large town they entered possessed the usual residences here and the work places there. But that's not what grabbed his attention. Not like the walled fortress on the hill that stood guard.

Rustom approached down the aisle. "Locals refer to the astounding color those fortress bricks produce as Honey Gold."

Crayle nearly repressed a response.

"Butterscotch."

"Ah, such as the flesh of your beloved spouse."

The Parsi's tone of voice didn't go over well. It betrayed the man's attraction to Hekka.

Crayle's mind shifted. He missed her tremendously. And checking his Smartphone would be fruitless. It was he who turned his comms dark.

CHAPTER 25

For Mag Crayle, the following scene must've been a dream. No. An absolute nightmare.

"My name is Nattie. And I appreciate your assistance on this very important matter, Mr. Crayle. I shall express my copious gratitude up front."

"Perhaps I could be of even more assistance were I not tethered to this chair."

She only smiled at his comment, and moved on.

"I'll tell you what I know. You can fill in the blanks." She smiled. With the selfsame point dimples of her sibling. "Pattie, my sister, was born of her prostitute mother in Amsterdam during a client visitation. As identical twins, the researchers only needed one of us to study."

"They?"

"The Aryans. It was their miscreant research doctor, Kaari Mengele, following in the footsteps of her well-known great grandfather,

Joseph, with such wicked science. But, back to my purpose today. Tell me what I don't know."

Crayle knew the story could take a while. And, the longer it took, the better chance he had to be rescued. The plethora of his knowledge regarding the deceased rogue CIA psychopath gave him a bizarre form of comfort. He began. "Pattie spent her early years at her mother's brothel. She responded to not having a father present like so many, except she didn't fall into drugs or minor crime."

"It was worse?"

"Homicide. She murdered. Starting with your mother's clients. The ones who abused your mother."

"She brought justice."

"That's how it started."

"I can tell from your inflection. That's not where it ended."

"It is said that revenge tastes sweet. There's a serious difference between justice and revenge. She invented ways to make death more painful. And less immediate."

"I see. That's where it went."

Crayle nodded at the teapot. "More?"

She nodded back, still mesmerized by her pensive thoughts.

"She started to enjoy it."

Nattie reacted. She seemed particularly impacted by that reality.

He responded. "It hit you, too, didn't it? The psychosis was embedded in your genes."

"I conclude that the evil Doctor Mengele initiated gene editing. Our mother may have been Subject One. Unaffected, herself, but supplying the inevitably homicidal traits to Pattie … and me."

Crayle was assaulted by an epiphany. A means of prolonging the dialog, and, likely, his life.

"What if it could be reversed?"

Her mind had drifted. His last statement snapped her back. "You could do that? Would do that? For me?"

"I know someone. Quite well. He'd take this on in an instant."

Crayle's second thoughts were immediate. Nattie could kill Doctor Rorschach in a heartbeat. Over time, the doctor's efforts at mind manipulation had progressed from ancillary to pivotal with regard to the CIA's operational efficacy. He was now requisite, and Crayle needed to take the greatest care in offering patient Nattie to him.

As if she'd read his thoughts, she responded to them. "You worry. And with cause. I could kill your resource just for the pure pleasure of it, and, in the process, destroy what is likely my only hope."

"I knew your sister that well."

Nattie dropped deep into considering a new way forward. Relief from her psychosis. From the killing. From the elation. From the pain.

She offered a brief smile, keeping the dimples at bay. "I'll do my part."

She walked to him, the knife still in her hand, and cut Crayle free.

The action dumped him into a quandary. He could leap at her. Relieve her of the weapon, using the nervous system-centric techniques he'd learned from Ling, and end it right then and there. Or, choose the highly dangerous alternate route. Put her together with the doctor.

He chose the latter.

"I'll work with you, Nattie. You have my word."

She pushed out a guarded smile. It spoke volumes about the galaxy of thoughts whirling through her mind.

"One more thing. The person who initiated all of this personal torture and mayhem? Doctor Kaari Mengele. She died in the red caverns the Aryan Alliance utilized as a base of operations. Beneath the Disney-like, fairy-tale castle in Southern Bavaria."

"Was it violent?"

"It was."

"I wish I could've been there."

Crayle considered what he'd just heard. He imagined a job seeking resume. "Effusively psychotic." He shook the mental dalliance from his consciousness.

He was jolted back into the present. Nattie went to her knees before him. Softly, and with gentle precision, she levered his knees apart. She straightened, and touched her lips to his.

Before he could react, Nattie reached up and around, pressed the knife blade against the back of his neck, just above the hairline, and made the slightest of cuts. A thumb push on the upper tab of the weapon's protective upper hilt. A small portion of liquid entered the miniscule wound.

As soon as he lost consciousness, she departed.

CHAPTER 26

The southbound Hyper Hummer transporting Hekka, Phoebe, and Lenny headed toward the well-known Silk Road town of Turpan from the Xinjiang province capitol, Ürümqi. It was late afternoon, the sun exiting stage West to their right.

Arzu, the Uighur guide, was into play-by-play. "We head south-south-east, past the East end of the Tien Shan mountain range. The distance is about sixteen miles and should take no more than a half-hour. Today's destination, Turpan, holds many interesting facets."

"Interesting, did you say?" Hekka recalled the ancient Asian curse, 'May you live in interesting times.'

Arzu glanced over, and continued. "We'll spend the night, and depart westward in the morning."

"Destination?"

"It's called Kucha. 120 or so miles from here, but more notably halfway along the Northern Silk Road. The ancient road spread into two to avoid, top and bottom, the unforgiving Taklamakan Desert. Your ancestors would have avoided it, as well. The county of Turpan is the driest of all China. Nearly 300 dry days per year. Water is a critical substance."

Hekka nodded appreciation of Arzu detailing the relevance of everything to her quest.

The Uighur was informative, but curious as well.

"Please tell me, Misses Crayle. When did you marry … and where?" She hoped her formal reference would elicit a *just-call-me-Hekka* entreaty to friendship.

Hekka considered a basic lie. That they'd grabbed a plane to Las Vegas, and simply gotten hitched. No unpaid witnesses to explain. That would put to bed any further discussion on the subject. A clever way out intervened. The truth.

"Well, we were married, along with two other couples, in a beautiful cathedral."

"I've seen pictures of their beautiful stained glass. Of cathedrals. Go on, please."

"Here's the exciting part. And please save your questions for when I'm finished."

A nod.

"It was 300 feet beneath the city we call Washington, D.C. A wonderful ceremony. The man presiding was the President of the United States. And the one performing the ritual was … the Pope."

"No one would believe that. Why did you …" Arzu let out a hearty laugh. Then, "It's the American sense of humor. I must learn it from you on this trip. For when I travel to your country some day. After Xinjiang independence."

Oh, shoot, Hekka thought. She reminded herself. Spies must take care not to add friends. Arzu was a top candidate, though, if that caveat ever ceased to exist.

Tired from the flight, they'd hopped into the super jeep, and left Ürümqi. The speech Ling asked her to give as payment for the empress' help was supposed to happen tomorrow. Back in the capitol.

"We have to go back!"

"To Hong Kong?"

"Ürümqi! I have a speech to give tomorrow!"

"It's okay. Empress Ling told me you'd give some sort of speech for her. I responded that our trip requires coordinating with locals along the way. She understood. And postponed your talk. When we finish out West, you are to use the phone number she supplied. We'll fly back to the capitol, you'll speak, we'll say goodbye, then back to Hong Kong for you."

"Thank you, Arzu. That's a load off my shoulders."

The Uighur laughed at the visual in her mind.

"That wasn't an American joke, just a saying."

The girl stopped. "A saying?"

"We'll work on jokes and sayings along the way. By the time our trip is through, you'll be an expert."

As the quartet passed a trellis, Arzu pulled over and snatched a stem full with ripe grapes, offering half to her client. "Try them. Turpan is renowned in Asia for its grapes.

Hekka popped in one at a time figuring, as she did, that travelers in ancient times did the same.

"Mmmm. Delicious. Very sweet. Not bitter at all."

"It's the weather, and the waters. Plenty of sun. We don't get much precipitation here in the Tarim Basin. But from the narrow Tien Shan range along the North side, and Tibetan flow from the South, we get plenty of water. It all makes for an extended season without frost."

"That explains the high sugar content. And it sounds like we shouldn't be impeded on our journey by snow or ice."

"Just so."

• • •

Morning, as it'd done for many millennia, came to Turpan. Before seeking their rooms the previous evening, the quartet scheduled a breakfast session for the next day. Their next stop, Kucha, was a bit distant. They'd need to leave early to avoid the mid-day sun.

Hekka and Arzu arrived early for breakfast. They chatted casually until interrupted.

Phoebe had apparently rousted Lenny from a fitful sleep. Hekka could tell. The two entered the kitchen area and headed their way. He feigned rubbing his eyes to indicate that his slumber had been deep, and peaceful, until she showed up. In case that wasn't enough, and his misery underestimated, he punctuated the scene with his usual, "Whine."

Arzu turned. "He wants wine with his breakfast?"

"It's a different word. Sounds the same. I'll explain later."

Crisis abated, Arzu decided to use the time for a brief lay-of-the-land lecture. "We have many deserts in Central Asia. Taklamakan here in Xinjiang. Kyzylkum in Uzbekistan. Karakum in Turkmenistan. Thar Desert in northwest India. And many more. Your ancestors would have been familiar with desert life, and its dangers. Do you have such lands where you're from?"

"We do. Nearby to our elevated Big Bear Valley is the large, Mojave Desert."

Arzu surmised. "It could be a link."

CHAPTER 27

While Phoebe and Lenny left ostensibly to survey the territory and ensure security, Hekka and her new friend and guide, Arzu, launched into in-depth conversation regarding their mutual tribal provenances. After about twenty minutes, Phoebe returned, pecking on her Smartphone.

Hekka scanned the room. "Where's Lenny?"

Phoebe seemed to know. "Oh, I ran into him in the bathroom a while ago. Standing at the toilet. All I saw was his back."

"And ..."

"He heard me. He said, 'I'm done. Just securing my weapon.' Then, he put out that laugh that drives everyone crazy. I said, 'Oh, your pee shooter."

She got the chuckle. Mostly from Arzu.

"You didn't harm him, Phoebe?" Hekka asked.

"No. He elbowed his way past, and said he had something to take care of. Out the door he went."

"Was he armed?"

"He had his Walther PPK in a shoulder holster. Under that ugly jacket he wears."

"If he had a jacket, how ..."

"Because ill-fitting cheap shoulder holsters show ... to the trained eye." She didn't mention that her training was as an FBI Agent.

Just then, Arzu heard something outside. She rushed to the window, and peaked past the drawn curtain.

"Oh, my!" She slapped her hand over her mouth.

The other two ran to see what crisis she'd witnessed.

There was Lenny. Running full bore down the street toward them. Behind, a squadron of saffron-garbed Buddhists in hot pursuit.

Phoebe threw out a ballpark estimate. "There's gotta be fifty of them!"

"Quick!" Hekka ordered. "Front porch!"

In a couple of seconds, that's where they stood.

Lenny was now twenty yards distant.

Closing fast.

The diminutive P.I. pulled up in front of the three women, now elbow to elbow.

Phoebe had her .45 caliber Glock 30 drawn, its side pressed against her chest.

Hekka likewise gripped her ten-inch Bowie knife.

Arzu, apparently unarmed, stepped forward.

Lenny took the place she'd vacated in the center of the line, spun on his heel, and adopted a taunting glare.

The Buddhists pulled up ten feet away.

Arzu was magnificent. She handily threw out various relevant teachings of the Buddha, admonishing the priests for even considering violence.

Hekka contributed, too. She plucked a wad of local currency from her purse, and offered alms to the leader of the pack. For the cause.

As one the troupe bowed, wheeled right, and headed back toward their temple.

The four watched until the Lenny-generated adversaries meandered out of sight, then stepped inside.

Phoebe was first. "So, Lenny. What did you do? Show them your weapon?"

"*Jeez-Louise.*" He shook his head. "I didn't even get that far. I entered their temple to get directions. To the 7/11. Before I could speak, that lead guy said a word I understood. It prompted a joke. I told it. That's all."

"That explains their instant conversion to violence after how many thousands of years?"

"What did you say, Lenny?" Arzu asked.

"I said, if you're gonna have a Near Vanna, you gotta have a Far Vanna. I put on my moves. And rapped it. Then, of course, I laughed."

Hekka headed them toward the kitchen. "C'mon, guys. Let's get some grub."

"And drink," Phoebe added.

• • •

Refueled, the group walked out to their 'monster' vehicle, and headed West. To Kucha.

CHAPTER 28

The trio of Crayle, Micmac, and the Parsi escaped the turmoil of attempting to smuggle miniaturized nuclear bombs in through the southeast Iran port of Bandar Beheshti. Time to thank lucky stars, then contrive a means of accomplishing the same effect without the risk of internment in an Iranian prison.

"Good morning, Mr. Crayle."

The bright face peering down on him was that of Rustom Modi. The shaking back and forth and bouncing up and down was courtesy of what must have been a first generation Indian bus.

It was clear that the near disaster of the previous day colluded with the rock of the boat to have placed him into a fitful sleep. It's why he didn't remember coming ashore, saying goodbye, or anything else.

Crayle rubbed his eyes to ensure he could see signs of life rather than pinch himself to ensure that he was still alive.

"We'll grab breakfast in Jaisalmer," said the happy face. "Then, a long trek northward."

"We're back in India?"

"North of Rapur, where we picked up our boat. Uh …" He calculated. "500 kilometers or so." He pointed to the rear of the bus. "That way."

Crayle converted. "About 310 miles."

"Off to your left, the border with Pakistan. This road runs parallel, but keeps a safe distance. Eighty kilometers or so." Rustom tilted his head slightly. "Fifty miles?"

"May I assume after our near disaster yesterday, you're attempting what American footballers call an *end around*?"

"We do get your television feed in our India provinces, Mr. Crayle. I do know the term. And, yes, my Plan B has us coming in, are you ready, the back door to Iran."

"I don't want to jump the gun, but having a Plan B implies you actually listened to my sage advice."

"My wife, Leonor, puts sage in my meals. Perhaps that was it." Rustom produced a wink and a smile. "We are headed to the North of this country. The Punjab/Kashmir region. A town called McLeod Ganj."

"So, where from McLeod Ganj?"

"I … we … have options. We could head West in this bus. Into Pakistan through Islamabad. Then, westward still through Kabul. You know, Afghanistan."

"Or …"

"Fly out from the airport in Gaggal near McLeod. A treacherous choice over those mountains this time of year."

"Versus Pakistan and Afghanistan. Here, let me flip a coin." He patted his pockets. "Do you have one? Not the same on both sides?"

• • •

The fort on the hill in Jaisalmer was legendary. Inside the walls, Rustom Modi led Crayle and Micmac to a favorite restaurant. FREE TIBET seemed like an unlikely name, but that was it. They were quickly seated inside, and took a minute or two to ensure themselves the place wouldn't jar them back and forth as in the bus.

"So, what's with your choice here? What do we need to know? Don't try the curry?"

"As you have seen by its sign, this is called the Free Tibet restaurant."

"Free Tibet?" Crayle pondered. "Let me check my schedule." He pretended tapping his Smartphone. "No new missions for us in less than a week."

"I'll pass on the humor. It's a restaurant. Tibetan, Indian, and Asian food. Freshly prepared. Here, I'll order a smattering."

He waved over the waiter.

"Sir?"

"Plates of the delicious chicken momos with the Everest Red Chili Sauce. Plus some of the Veg Thukpa. And Kingfisher beer times three."

"Yes, Mr. Modi," the waiter responded before he hustled off. He returned with the sumptuously aromatic meal in short order.

The trio spent their time eating, and regarding the scenery. Especially, the gold fortress surrounding them.

Finished, the Americans glanced at Rustom as if to ask, "What's next?"

"I'll pay the check," the Parsi announced.

Micmac had enjoyed the food too much. "How about a swim off for the check."

"This is desert. Although Winter temperatures range here from 41 degrees to about 75 degrees Fahrenheit, we only get .05 inches of rain this time of year."

"Back to the sea, then. A six mile swim off," said the former SEAL.

"You'd have to come back and save me before too long."

"Yell loud enough. I'll do just that."

"And carry me back to shore?"

"Naw. Tote you along for the rest of the six miles."

"You'd do that?"

"Yeah. Slow me down a bit. But, yeah."

"You appear physically, and in your moves, to be quite an athlete. Mr. Micmac, if we finish by February, you might return here for the annual camel races. To take part."

"Let's stay on mission here, Rusty. Something you should know. Rest assured. We SEALS don't leave anyone behind. For example, imagine if one of your devices detonates prematurely. I'd scour all of India and the Middle East to find every last part."

"I feel reassured," Rusty acknowledged.

Crayle rained on the parade.

"At 8,000 degrees Fahrenheit, good luck with that."

They all had a chuckle, then Rustom paid the bill, and led them back to the bus.

• • •

Replete with sustenance to carry them forward, the team departed Jaisalmer on its way north to McLeod Ganj.

"I hope everyone enjoyed the repast in Jaisalmer. Perhaps you'll return someday. With spouse. With children. But we can not delay. We have a schedule to keep. We'll arrive in McLeod this evening. So get sleep, play video games, and check out the magazines in the seat back pouches. They are a bit used, but have some really great pictures. I'll help if you have difficulties with any of the words in Hindi."

After what seemed like eons, the dilapidated bus trundled into McLeod in northern India. As anticipated, the view in the distance gave up tall mountains. The Himalayas of Tibet were not far.

As if a mind reader, Modi passed out quilted parkas to the two Americans.

"We'll not be here long. When our jet arrives and refuels, we go. To arrive in our target destination in a manner that won't, and can't, be anticipated."

"So we fly over the high mountains, with guaranteed turbulence. With two devices that aren't the most stable to begin with," Crayle observed. "Explain the trip out in a little more detail, Rusty,"

"Life's about risks, Mr. Crayle."

Micmac entered the fray. "A bumpy plane ride has to be better than this bus."

Rustom Modi fixed him with a stare. "Wanna bet?"

After the brief respite, the bus deposited the trio in McLeod's Tibetan temple.

"Can't we just drive to the airport, and get going?"

"There's someone you need to meet first."

Rustom led them inside and past several imposing security guards.

A tall thin man pulled open an ornate, heavy door for them.

Inside, they surveyed a large room as extravagantly decorated as humanly possible. That wasn't what grabbed Crayle's attention.

It was the old thin man sitting cross-legged on a large pillow across the room. Two jaws dropped.

"Some background is in order," said Modi in as soft a voice as he could muster. "Some time ago, China reasserted its claim to Tibet. To insure his safety, the Dalai Lama was brought here. McLeod Ganj has been the seat of the Lama ever since."

"We have a meet with the Dalai Lama," Crayle uttered.

"Yes. He has something to ask of you."

"Of me? What ..."

"Mr. Crayle," emanated from the religious icon. "I hear your schedule is tight, as they say. I shall be brief. We live here in comfort, but still in exile. My understanding is that you have the ear of the empress of all of China."

Crayle cast a glance at Rustom, who just tilted his head at the speaker.

"I wish you to intercede on our behalf. We want our country back. In return, safe passage to you three while in Central Asia."

A bell rang, and the doorman ushered them out. Before returning inside, he handed them a scroll. The large door closed without a sound.

Rustom advised. "He never grants audiences. He really wants Tibet back."

"I don't believe I have that much influence with Ling. If and when we get through this, I'll give it a try."

"And, successful or not, we've got a scroll from the Lama. Get Out Of Jail Free."

"Cute," Crayle responded. Then, "Rusty?"

"Hmmm?"

"The airport?"

CHAPTER 29

After the rescue of their errant compatriot from the outraged Buddhists, Lenny, Hekka, along with Arzu and Phoebe, proceeded away from Xinjiang's oasis town, Turpan, heading West along the main highway. She'd eaten some tasty fare and wished she could've enjoyed it along with husband, Magus. He was probably stuck in Washington, D.C.

She thought it would've been far nicer having him along to share experiences instead of him scribbling on and pushing a raft of boring government documents around on his new, boring government desk at Langley.

She checked her Smartphone. No comms. She considered trying to circumvent the blackout, but decided no. The attempt would no doubt be noticed by some bureaucratic types who needed something, anything, to latch onto. They could cause grief at least a thousand times worse than any imagined transgression. Best to avoid.

Their next destination along the Northern Silk Road popped into view.

There they were. In their second major Silk Road town, Kucha, Xinjiang, China. Hekka, Phoebe, Lenny, and guide Arzu arrived from Turpan to seriously begin their team leader's research.

Arzu was ready with the dialog. "The range of mountains running East-West on the North side of this town, Kucha, is the Tien Shan I mentioned before. The range runs all the way ahead to our border with the Stans."

Lenny was quip on the uptake.

"Stans? Like in Laurel and Hardy?"

Arzu kept her eyes on the road. But deftly delivered a comeback.

"You know. Kazakh*stan*, Kyrgyz*stan*, Tajiki*stan*, Uzbeki*stan*, Turkmeni*stan*. Central Asia. With Afghani*stan* and Paki*stan* below them, sandwiched in between Iran and India."

"It sounds like Stan means Land Of," Hekka posited.

"Nicely done, Mrs. Crayle. You'll make a fine professor."

"Please, call me Hekka. We're old friends by my measure."

She wasn't going to miss the opportunity. Most spies weren't around anyone long enough to establish, let alone maintain, friendships. That she and Magus had fellow covert operators, the MacKays and Lipschitzes, as friends for over three years now seemed like a blessing.

"By the way," Arzu interrupted. "A little known fact. Under Mongol dominance, the Xinjiang of old was known as Uighuri*stan*."

"Should I ever require a dissertation for my professorship, I'll have that tidbit of knowledge in reserve."

Arzu smiled. A building was constructed using a number of nails. Not just one. She felt she'd added even more certainty to the notion of a long-term friendship with the American.

The Hummer pulled into a large hotel labeled Kuche International Hotel. Arzu didn't explain the apparent misspelling of the city's name. Hekka let it slide.

Once checked in, Arzu gathered the entourage in a sitting area for a brief lecture.

"Kucha, oh, about 2,000 years ago, was the largest of the 36 kingdoms in this part of the world. Now, it sits on the Tarim

Highway, the longest road ever built across a desert. We're lucky. It's been relatively mild on our journey. The Winter temperature in Kucha has been recorded below minus twenty degrees Fahrenheit."

Lenny, for his part, sat leaning against a wall in his parka, shivering for effect.

"Thank you, Mr. Lipschitz, for your enactment."

"Yeah. You're welcome. But, look, if it's all the same, I'm going to my room and get some sleep." Without waiting for a response, he left.

"Well, there's a mosque to see, and a famous tomb, but I'm afraid it will get a lot colder outside. We'll get some food, some sleep, and head out in the morning."

"To the mosque and the tomb?"

"To the caves. There's artwork left there from long, long ago. You need to see it."

They group chowed down on kebabs, naan bread, melons, and other local fare before turning in for the night. Tomorrow was another day. They didn't know it at the time. But, one hell of another day.

CHAPTER 30

Out bright and early with her charges, Arzu took the lead as she drove them the forty-three miles northwest from Kucha to their destination. She engaged them with a built-in intercom.

"The Kizil Caves and their artifacts have been studied for hundreds of years. It is sad that archaeologists sought to preserve, by removing, what ancient types created. They put their lives and beliefs into art, making money and reputation in the process."

"There must be some things left to see, or you wouldn't bring me there."

"Yes. We'll get to that, Hekka. First, we're stopping here."

She stopped the vehicle in the middle of the dirt road.

Lenny piped up, for a change. "You're blocking the road. Is there somewhere to pull off?"

"Please be silent, Mr. Lipschitz. We are the only visitors permitted this day. I made arrangements before leaving Hong Kong."

That pronouncement indicated to FBI Agent Phoebe that everything was to be to schedule. No surprises. Good.

The team followed the Uighur out along a path. Hekka's initial uneasy feeling regarding the landscape escalated the farther they walked.

On each side were cliffs. Wedge-shaped cliffs. Ever narrowing, wedge-shaped cliffs. It seemed a real-life replay of her video AI experience back at the cabin. But how could anyone know what would befall her on her research trip. At times, coincidences occur, she reasoned. She shook if off. It was that, or go stark raving mad.

Through the ever-narrowing gap, Arzu held up a balled fist to bring her group to a halt.

There, dead ahead, flowed an enthralling beauty of nature.

"It's called The Spring Of Tears. As you might guess, there's a story behind the name." She then related a story fitting for only the most touching of romance novels. Love … and Tragedy encapsulated.

"Stop sniffling, Lenny," Phoebe ordered, so as to mask her own emotional response to what she'd just heard.

Hekka added, "The story is one we can all feel, as much as hear."

Arzu nodded. "Yes. So, follow me back. On … to the Caves."

• • •

The Kizil Caves were impressive even from the outside. Temple-like structures were engraved into the side of the vertical cliff facing them.

The team followed their guide to an opening.

"This is cave number … I have it here somewhere." She searched to no avail. "No matter. I know this cave. It is one with intact art. Beware that, once inside, there will be echoes that are quite loud. They can even obscure what is being said. Speak softly," she glanced at Lenny, "or perhaps not at all."

"Whine," Lenny replied.

They trailed behind Arzu.

Caves have a habit of being wet, cold, and dark. This one didn't disappoint. Especially since they were in the foothills of the Tien Shan mountain range in early Winter.

As they proceeded, motion sensitive lights flicked on, although muted in brightness. Still, enough light so the group could see rectangular sections on the caves' walls where ancient art existed, but had been removed and carried off by archaeologists, or less scrupulous thieves.

Hekka, Phoebe, and Lenny kept close behind Arzu as she led them deeper into the cave catacombs. They reached a stretch where the motion sensor lights didn't respond.

Their guide whispered. "Every once in a while, a segment of lights fails. It's normal."

She reached a spot where the cave tunnel curved sharply right, and led them around.

Up ahead in the distance, they saw a shimmering light.

There appeared to be motion.

Just then, a new set of lights flashed on.

Overhead.

Now everyone could see.

Five men busied themselves trying to remove a painting from the tunnel wall. They'd been prescribed the acceptable procedures by a museum in Berlin that had history with this sort of thing.

The men, who expected no one on this day due to their normally reliable resource's information, scrambled for their AK-47s.

Phoebe had her .45 caliber Glock 30 out first.

She took the man who'd just flicked his safety.

A bullet right between the eyes. SOP for the one whose fellow FBI Agents referred to as Annie Oakley.

The hit caused muscles to contract. As the dead man fell, the AK's bullets sprayed everywhere. He nailed two of his own before the firing ceased.

The reverberant sounds in the caves resembled a chorus of several jackhammers at full throttle.

A fusillade from Hekka, Arzu, and Lenny took down the final two thieves.

There was complete silence when all was done.

An ejected casing from Lenny's Walther PPK had landed on a ledge. It fell with a *tink, tink, tink.*

"Anyone hit?" Phoebe queried.

"No," the others responded.

After that, it was just breaths.

Seconds seeming like minutes passed.

Then, Arzu retook the lead.

"Just to the right of them is a well. We'll dump the bodies, and put their weapons and ammo in the duffel I brought. With our water bottles."

"What happened here, Arzu?" Hekka asked. "Today was to be us only."

"I'm guessing. They had a resource somewhere that informed them the caves were closed. Wall art from ancient caves is nearly priceless. Especially in Europe. Those who gorge themselves on the profits rationalize that they are saving the art. It's BS, of course."

Lenny nosed into the conversation. "I could use one of those weapons. I brought a handgun to a full-auto rifle fight."

"They're going to our freedom fighters, Lenny. Sorry."

"Whine," the PI responded as Arzu began grabbing weapons and dumping bodies.

The others pitched in.

As a final task, the team collected the multitude of shell casings flung in all directions by the automatic and semi-automatic weapons. The projectile pock marks weren't even noticeable due to the rough texture of the cave walls.

No one would ever suspect what just happened.

Finished inside with both the pick up activities and a view of the art, the group retreated to the entrance. Arzu stopped there, and turned. “I’ll call for a clean up.”

With reception back above zero, she did.

That done, they reloaded themselves into the Hummer.

“We’ll catch a little rest at a smallish hotel right nearby. I’ll make sure things get completed at the cave. Tomorrow, we’re headed West. I promise, to the degree I can, no more extra-curricular activities.”

Lenny finished it off. “Definitely E-ticket! Take that, Mr. Toad’s Wild Ride!”

CHAPTER 31

The team of three, replete with two mini-nukes disguised as rugby balls, checked out of North India's Dalai Lama haven, McLeod Ganj, and into the nearby town of Gallal with its regional airport. As planned, the CIA's off-the-books Dassault Falcon 9X was refueled and waiting. The pilot, Brazil-sexy Flori, welcomed them aboard.

Boarding first, former sailor Micmac stowed his luggage and garnered a table. Starboard side. Mid-ship. He checked the view through the window, then waved Crayle and the Parsi, Rustom Modi, to their seats.

Crayle waxed wistful as he imagined watching the other Falcon—the one carrying Phoebe, Lenny, and Hekka—taxi away.

He wished to hell he'd been able to see Hekka off at Jack's international airport. Just giving her a long kiss, a tight hug, then a wave and a smile goodbye were standard operating procedure for situations like that.

His imagination conjured the rest of the scene. He'd give a brief hug to Lenny, their diminutive private investigator turned spy and true wild card, who to everyone's amazement came through big time on several occasions. Still, Team Crayle's resident pain-in-the-ass. The third and final member of Hekka's entourage, Phoebe, would apply her skills as protector by nature and by trade, assuring Hekka's safety though nothing untoward was anticipated on this research trip.

His final thought in this respect concluded that an imaginary sendoff falls far short of real-life seeing, and touching, and feeling.

He missed her a lot.

Micmac saw his expression. "You have one fine woman there, Mag."

"She's latched onto this quest of hers and, if I know her at all, she won't let go. We may have to run our little capers going forward with Hekka on extended leave from the Company."

The sailor nodded. He knew Crayle was right.

Crayle turned to the Parsi.

"So, Rusty, how are we going to get all those Grand Ayatollahs running Iran, and their minions, to turn it over to you. So you can resurrect Persia?"

Before he could respond, the intercom interrupted. "Buckle Up!"

He heard the three tail-mounted engines spin up.

"I don't like these belts. That's why there were none in the bus."

"Could've used 'em," Micmac replied. "Here you're in Flori territory. There's a head right back there." He pointed aft. "You don't buckle, she flushes you down the toilet."

Rusty scoffed. "I'd never fit through that little hole."

"This isn't your ordinary Dassault Falcon. It has mods. And, yes, you would fit."

The Parsi considered the implication. Micmac seemed to be saying that he was sure, because it'd been done.

He buckled up.

Crayle brought them back to the reason they travelled on the jet in the first place. The mission ahead.

"First, let's rehash one of our past successes."

He had their attention.

"A while back, a bomb was smuggled into the Muslim neighborhood of Marseilles, and detonated. Made it look like extremists had The Bomb."

The other two relaxed with their drinks. And listened.

"It followed a similar explosion, same footprint, as the first mini-nuke in Central Iran. So, you get the tie in."

Rustom caught the drift. "No one will be surprised, then, if one goes off in Tehran."

"That is correct. Getting it there is the challenge we face."

"Yes. We must get the leaders, except for their Number One, Jahni, into a government building."

"We must get the civilians away from Tehran!"

"That would be Item Two, Rusty."

"And I must finish it all in the ancient Persian capitol far from Tehran. In the far southwest of the country."

"That's where you'll make your victory speech."

"It sounds so simple."

"Don't kid yourself. It's quite complex. Fortunately, I have the chops, as Micmac would say, and a graduate level education in Systems Methodology to back that up."

• • •

Upon permission from the tower, Flori taxied the plane, and had them aloft in fifteen minutes. She clicked the intercom.

"We're heading northwest from Gallal Airport. We'll scoot over the Kunlun and then the Pamir Mountain ranges in order to stay out of Pakistan and Afghanistan air space. But, there's a possibility of weather coming in over those hills, so we may need a Plan B."

Rustom appeared puzzled. "Plan B? I'm losing track of plan this and that. Aren't we on Plan B?"

"In Flori's frame of reference, we're on Plan A. She doesn't know about our aborted Plan A at Bandar Beheshti. It's called compartmentalization. Need to know, and all that."

"Good. You have a knack for this, Mr. Crayle. You can keep organized. I and Mr. Micmac will focus on whichever is current."

"There you go, Rusty. Now, that's a plan."

The Parsi grabbed his head.

"*Ahhh!*"

• • •

They flew for a couple of hours. The view of the jagged, snow-capped mountains was spectacular.

The intercom intervened once more.

"Weather update. Having to divert northeast. Not to worry. Land. Get some fuel. Then, on from there. And remember. Buckle up is not an option."

The three couldn't see her, but could feel her smile.

CHAPTER 32

Jack Sommers, unable so far to find his replacement at the head of the Strategic Solutions Office or its super-ordinate organization, the Other Specialized Staffs office, found himself playing both full-time roles. Today was another one when he performed his third effort, requiring at least ten times the effort of the other two combined, as protem DCI at the CIA.

Down in the Washington, D.C. bowels once again. He smiled at his characterization as indicating there was a whole lot of crap going on in D.C. "How true, how true," he muttered.

The only other resident of the deep underground STIF room, one President of the United States, Kimbel Stones, responded.

"You just wandered off, Jack. I bet you were reminiscing about the fine state of affairs in this fine city."

"Something like that."

"Time for Global Sitrep II. Give it to me. And make it quick. I've got a meet with the new president of Cuba in thirty."

"Okay, here's what I have. Queen of Sweden. No political moves yet on our friend and asset, the new King Louis XX in France. Stability on that front."

"I like him being the Symmetric King. Based on the XX."

"They started that nomenclature with his dad. King Louis XIX."

"Yes. For some reason, I miss ole Sylvain Lalumière. Quite the adversary."

"Next up, Czarina Anastasia. She's built up Saint Petersburg as the new, or restored, capitol. No revolt over there. Her number one, that descendant of the mad monk, Rasputin, seems a little worn out, though."

"Anastasia is not just the Romanov heir. She's heir to Catherine the Great and her *modus operandi*."

"Since you brought in the Latin, Mr. President, I'll segue to the Pope. Something going on over there. Cardinals hustling in and out all the time. We watch, by the way, for normal traffic of all sorts to become abnormal. Anyway, we're keeping an eye out. Not long ago, the world lost the previous Pope as well as that Grand Ayatollah heading the religious government in Iran. Neither one to natural causes, by the way."

"They weren't very nice guys. I believe the Creator had his way with them."

"That would be *she*, Mr. President."

"If it were *she*, *she'd* be blamed for all the turmoil and mayhem over the millennia. I'm going with *he*."

"As you wish, Sire."

"Hmmm. If I didn't need you so badly, Jack ..."

"That you do works for me."

"To that end, and I mean end, where's my new DCI?"

"Oh, I almost forgot. Stuff going on the South coast area of Iran. Probably nothing. A big to do about a boat coming in from Mumbai, India. Via Pakistan. Probably nothing."

"So, where in the world is Mag Crayle?"

The president glanced wistfully at the ceiling.

"To that, I've been in touch with a Central Asian asset. Says Hekka, his wife, is still crossing Xinjiang on her research quest. Seems Mag's still dark. No contact at all."

"I know quite well that Hekka's his wife, Jack. What I don't know … is where the hell is Mag."

CHAPTER 33

On the road, and putting Kucha and the Kizil Caves in the rearview mirror, Hekka and her team relaxed. She got her fill of observing the dramatic landscape with the mountain range on the right and vast desert on the left. It was time to find out a little more from her Uighur-Mongol guide.

"How about your ethnic background, Arzu. Please tell me … if you feel comfortable talking about it."

Arzu, who drove the Hummer and encountered no challenges requiring singular focus on the excellent Tarim Highway, responded to Hekka's comment.

"Yes. My mother is Mongol. She traces back to Genghis Khan and his Golden Horde."

"Tough lady?"

An affirmative nod, and a minimalist smile.

Hekka noted the muted expression so characteristic of her own upbringing. *Keep emotions in check* was the unspoken mantra. In spite of her own parents' geographic disparity, Southern California to Finland, the Serrano and Finns were closely aligned regarding emotion suppression. To see this in someone half a world away established a connection between the two women.

"There's a common bond here. Our heritage … our kindred heritage … bonds us. I feel it."

"I feel it, too."

"And there's a title for one of your husband's future spy novels."

"Which is?"

"The Kindred Heritage."

Hekka smiled. She felt the warmth of her new friend.

Arzu smiled back. Then, returned to the job at hand.

"Come. We go."

They reached the outskirts of a sizeable city.

"Here we are entering Kashgar. We'll stop at this restaurant. There is someone you need to meet to continue your quest. She's Aziza. Uighur-Uzbek. From Uzbekistan."

As soon as Arzu had the mega-Hummer parked, the team exited and headed for the door. Lenny had the first impression.

"Hey! Check it out! I missed out at our first city. But look at this. Another FUBAR. Must be a chain. Maybe they got T-shirts."

Phoebe, as usual, had an opinion. "Well, if it says FUBAR on the front, and you promise to wear it, I'm buying."

"Did you hear that? Phoebe promised to do something nice."

The other three properly ignored the comment and headed inside. Arzu spoke to the hostess, who seated them with a taller and slightly thinner woman who sported waist-length black hair just like Hekka's. Lenny and Phoebe sat at a table for two nearby. Arzu made the introductions. First, the team, then, "This is Aziza."

The waitress arrived. Apparently, Lenny was not seated far enough away from the others.

"You have Western food here. Good. That way I won't have to eat bugs." His laugh caught the attention of the other patrons.

Arzu and Aziza shared a glance. The look said they considered taping Lenny to his chair, and then forcing bugs—live bugs—down his throat.

Instead, the woman-in-charge continued where she'd left off.

"As you've already realized, Central Asia was populated by numerous nomadic tribes, many of which garnered regional power for periods of time. But always gave way to change."

"What about the mixing of ethnicities?"

Aziza, the Uighur-Uzbek, answered. "It happened. Children were generated that were at once seen as impure. Not full-blooded. But intriguing."

Hekka thought of her own wonderful daughter, Kianna. She quickly re-focused. "How did you two bi-ethnic women meet? It seems unlikely, given the demographics."

"There's an organization. On the Net."

That surprised Hekka. "I didn't know." She fished around in her purse. "Could you ..."

The Uzbeki pulled a small, metal Wellspring notebook from her bag, and jotted down the URL with a dot-org name, and handed it over.

Hekka regarded the name. "French," she said. "Vive La Différence. Long live the difference. I'll check it out. But right now, what's next, Arzu?"

"This city, Kashgar, sits at the confluence of pathways. The North and South renditions of the Silk Road diverge East from it, or converge West to it, skirting the formidable Taklamakan Desert, which comprises pretty much the Southern half of Xinjiang. The Northern route offered water and other respite from the heat, but was plagued by bandits. The South route provided a far safer transit, but the absence of water and the cold highlands of Tibet that bordered it on the South made the trip tough."

"What I'm gathering is that multitudes of peoples converged with their goods in Kashgar to begin their caravans East. To China."

"Yes. And that caused migration of peoples, some very much a mixture of races, that way."

"At some point, the mixing must've stopped. The indigenous of the Western Hemisphere arrived in tribes, each sporting similar characteristics."

"They then kept their DNA separated."

"That's what is believed. It explains the distinctive nature of the tribes as they migrated to Alaska and points South and East from there."

Hekka nodded agreement. "Over thousands of years. So people collected here. And from the Stans, from the Middle East, and ..."

"Yes. From India. The intermixing of those skin tonations provided a reddish hue to the natural brown."

"So, that coloring was not in evidence of the source ethnicities that supplied the components. The mixture occurred here, and moved East, then Northeast, and through China and Siberia to the Bering Land Bridge into today's Alaska."

"Everything we know fits that scenario. It's what scientists refer to as the behavioral theory. When all behaviors fit a theory, that validates the theory."

"It would be too much to find an example of those people in our indigenous predecessors in today's Central Asia. Right?"

"I thought you'd never ask. We need to go to my place here in Kashgar. I have things that may be of great interest to you."

With that, Aziza paid their checks, and they headed out.

CHAPTER 34

Less than ten minutes from the FUBAR restaurant, they arrived at Aziza's Kashgar home. The place was cozy with wood paneling and many decorative artifacts. She directed them to a sofa and chairs, the seating as comfortable as it appeared. She addressed the leader of the research team.

"Hekka, I found an interesting artifact during my own journey. It's believed to be from a tribe that migrated East through Siberia. Perhaps as far as the modern city called Irkutsk on Lake Baikal."

She pulled out the flat, wooden item perhaps eight inches by twelve inches.

"Check out this engraving, if that's the right word."

Hekka took it in her hands, and carefully examined it. She shared her observations.

"They put in all these symbols that are suggestive of the Western Hemisphere's so-called indigenous peoples." She pointed. "This one of a medicine man."

Her Uzbek guide watched and listened.

"You see here, Aziza," she continued. "It says **C-E-P-P-A-H-O**. If you say it out loud, *sep-ah-hoe*, it almost sounds like my native language."

• • •

Aziza showed Hekka, Arzu, Phoebe, and Lenny around her place. Replete with wood furniture and cushy pastel-print cushions, it had a particular warmth to it. It reminded Hekka of the style and substance back at her ranch house in Big Bear.

Hekka noticed something as she glanced down at her host's left hand. "No ring? Boyfriend?"

"I had one. After we got to know each other, he decided to refer to me in English, and to his friends, as Ooze Becky."

Phoebe, unaware of what passed for humor in this part of the world, decided to play. "Did they ever find the body?"

"Not all of it."

They all got the humor, and laughed.

The tension abated, Hekka turned to her guide.

"We call that Breaking The Ice, Arzu."

"They call that, Breaking The Ice, a saying, Aziza," Arzu explained.

Hekka brought them back on topic. "How about those who came before?"

"My Uzbeki ancestors were pushed out of Persia by the Arabians."

"So there's at least a trace of Persian blood in you."

"Yes. A trace. There's so much mixed ethnicity in our country, we could've been called Blenderstan. One of my ancestors collected artifacts. I want to show you these items. Is that okay?"

"It would be difficult for you to decide what might be important to me. I'll look."

Aziza walked to a large chest pushed against a wall. She produced a well-toned metal key, and opened it.

The two of them pieced through the contents. While the artifacts were of tremendous interest, none triggered a response in Hekka.

She leaned over the seemingly empty trunk. “There’s nothing left but this feather.” She lifted a six-inch long feather that had been pressed against the side by the more substantive items.

Hekka smiled at her guide, Aziza. “My own ancestors used feathers like this. For arrows.”

“I remember being told, that particular feather comes from a particular species of bird. Also used for arrows.”

Hekka’s face went blank. She spoke just above a whisper. “That’s the same bird.”

Arzu picked up the notion. “The lore here is that those migrations East collected the birds for their feathers, and took them along. In cages.”

“Then, they brought them across to Alaska and started populating the Americas. Over thousands of years.”

“Your link from here to there just became a lot stronger.”

Last, Aziza extracted a solid object covered in beautiful Chinese silk. The item was taped to prevent unraveling.

“Don’t open this now. It’s a gift. For when you arrive home.”

At that point, they packed up.

They headed for the airport. They thought.

CHAPTER 35

Aziza took a position facing her seated guests. She ignored Lenny as he fought a losing battle with his Smartphone.

"We are finished here. You've seen all I have. We now travel to a sight known as Shripton's Arch. I caution you ahead. We must beware of the flash floods. There are deep, narrow canyons leading to the arch."

She finished up by describing the absolute wonder of this natural formation.

They all padded out to their transportation, Aziza's four wheel drive. Phoebe pulled Lenny along by his elbow.

When they arrived, it was all she had said. Hekka felt as if the high, sheer wall closed in on her as the sunlight became more and more blocked. That the canyons were deep and narrow had been a gross understatement. It gave a shiver as had her experience earlier with Micmac's AI imaging software, and then for real just before the Kizil Kara Buddhist Caves. Brown sandstone had been Aziza's description. It was that.

When they reached a dead end, their guide stopped the vehicle, and all stepped onto the hard ground.

The troupe found it easy to whisper, and be heard.

Phoebe finally removed her hand from her Glock 30, and did so. "We should be safe here."

"If it rains," Aziza advised, "those rocks high above can come loose and fall. Although I've had good fortune, it would be hard to get out of their way. We must hurry forward to diminish the probability."

Hekka homed in on the last word. Whenever her husband, with his mathematical knowledge, used it, she knew she was in for a No Doz moment.

Where was he, anyway?

The group rounded a bend.

Then, there it was.

Magnificent. Surely worth the trip.

They consumed the sight of the 1,500 foot high arch with a gaping opening, estimated at 1,200 feet top to bottom, with enraptured wonder.

She was instantly inspired by nature's beauty. Even more so due to the appreciation of nature so characteristic of her Serrano tribe. Going forward the next days, she intended to bring her entire being into the speech in Ürümqi. Whatever Ling planned to be said, Hekka would deliver it with verve.

Then, another thought.

"Aziza? I've not had cell service for my phone since we've been here. Would those responsible for this arch mind if I climbed to the top of it? You know, to get bars."

She held her Smartphone aloft.

"I intend to drop all of you off at the airport for your trip back to the capitol. So … no."

She glanced around ready to stare down any dissent.

Only a soft whine sounded from Lenny.

"Back in the car, then. To the airport."

They heard thunder in the distance.

The corridor of solid, high canyon walls they'd driven between, added substantial emphasis.

"Quickly," Aziza urged.

"With luck, we'll beat the storm," Hekka added.

Back on the road, the Uzbek broke the unnerving silence.

She possessed a natural curiosity regarding new foreign words entering her sphere. "What is this word, *luck*?"

Hekka responded. "When some unexpected good comes to you or happens to you, not the consequence of something you did, we call that good luck."

"And if something bad happens?"

"That's bad luck. But only if you did nothing to cause it. It seems that success requires knowledge, skills, talent, and good luck."

"You are very wise."

She returned her minimalist smile. All four success components presented themselves at the Kizil Caves. They'd be dead otherwise. She thought of her husband. Her first notion, that he was at the moment sitting on a beach nursing an umbrella drink. More likely, he engaged himself in some sort of operation with the Parsi. She hoped to hell whatever he did was virtual and not *in situ*, like all of the other ops over the past three years. She felt confident he was safe.

The bad guys in his world were exceptionally bad. As is vying for bottom-of-the-barrel honors. He possessed the knowledge, skills, and talent to take them on. With the persistent good luck he'd enjoyed in the past, a single instance of bad luck could change it all. Silently, she prayed for his safety.

CHAPTER 36

Sadly for Hekka, it was time to bid adieu to Aziza, and travel back East to Ürümqi. The Uzbek said she had things to do, but would rather troop to the capitol and spend some time. So, it was just Hekka, Lenny, Phoebe, and Arzu. Marli had the Falcon 8X all fueled and ready. They still needed to pass through the terminal's bureaucracy.

Hekka stood at the end of the line at the airport's ticket counter with her roller suitcase ready to check in. With her very special TSA Pre-check designation for global travel, she was confident her loaded pistol and ten-inch Bowie knife would pass undetected.

She heard a voice from behind.

She spun on her heel.

It was him. Magus.

"How …"

He put a finger to his lips to hush her. He leaned close to whisper. "Not a word." Then, he nodded downward.

In his hand, concealed from others, his signature SIG-Sauer sidearm.

Pointed down.

She gave a start.

Crayle stuffed the pistol back inside his jacket. Into a shoulder holster.

Then … of course. It was her husband's way of telling her to make no noise. No scene.

Just then, Aziza returned from the bathroom. Spies needed to be resourceful. The Serrano spy was well-versed in that requirement.

"Oh," Hekka informed her. "I just ran into this American. From Kansas City."

Aziza just returned her glance with a knowing stare.

"You, you know him?"

"Not like that," said the Uzbek. "After we see you off, we're actually on our way West. On a mission."

Hekka felt her wrist pressing against the Bowie knife situated between her breasts. "You think it's all happened. That there'll be no more surprises."

At that point, Arzu returned from a visit to the airport's information booth. The Uighur spy spoke before Hekka could attempt another introduction.

"Oh, hi, Mag! I mean, you must be Mr. Crayle."

Her eyes moved back to Mr. Crayle's wife. The one from whose beautiful face the butterscotch tone had drained.

Hekka was not one to be devoid of either spirit or answers to obvious rhetorical questions. "I must return to Ürümqi. Marli has the jet ready. Come with me, Arzu. We need to talk."

Crayle motioned for them, all of them, to follow him.

At a door clearly marked *Do Not Enter!*, Crayle tapped in a code on a wall-mounted security device and received the expected *Click!*

He nodded the others through first, then descended the stairs ahead and out onto the tarmac.

Outside, he explained as he walked her past his nearly new Falcon 9X to her waiting older, and more experienced, Falcon 8X, its engines already spinning. She waved at Aziza, already on Flori's gangway, and blew her a kiss. As she turned away, she saw into the 9X windows the faces of the not too well known rock group and MI-6 black ops team, which called itself The Apostles. Matthew, Mark, Luke, and Jane. The ones her husband recently worked a successful op with in the Emirates. And a subsequent one on Portuguese territory.

She stopped at the foot of her gangway, giving her husband a kiss to remember.

Then, she followed Lenny, Phoebe, and Arzu aboard.

CHAPTER 37

With Hekka and crew now in the air and headed East, Crayle and team had climbed aboard their ride headed to and over the nearby Stans. Until they were seated and the pilot apprised them of a change of plans.

Flori informed her passengers that there was a problem with the 9X. Since they'd taken delivery of a new, but pre-production, version, it wasn't a surprise. They'd have to grab a train West and hopefully she'd catch up when the problem was solved.

They deplaned and were whisked to the train station and hopped aboard a somewhat dated train, which didn't appear too worn thin, and everyone, quite tired by now, didn't care. They hopped on board, found their overnight rooms and fell asleep in short order.

• • •

Crayle slept well. The clickety-clack of the train wheels and the swaying, as they passed out of the Tarim Basin of Xinjiang and through the mountain pass to the West, put him out and kept him that way for hours. Now, with sunlight peeking through not-so-blackout drapes, he came alive once more, prepared to face whatever lay ahead.

That remained the question. What lay ahead?

And what about Hekka? Being kept in the dark in need-to-know mode by one's own husband found disfavor from her. He could tell. Before he could dwell on that subject, a knock came at the door.

"It's open!"

The potential assailant tried.

Crayle popped onto the floor from his second tier perch. "Who's there?"

"Aziza … alone."

A couple of seconds later, they sat side-by-side on the bottom berth, the door closed and relatched.

"I slept fine, my Uzbek friend. What's ahead?"

"We're transiting Irkeshtam Pass. It's much more stable than Torugart Pass to the North. Still, stay seated or with both hands on something solid. The ride through can get exciting."

"Nothing like The White Horse Pass And Yukon Route Railroad up to the Canadian Yukon. There are places where the railroad builders fairly stapled the tracks to vertical walls of granite."

"Oh," said Aziza. "That sturdy?"

Just then, their car shook sideways with such violence that both were pitched onto the floor.

He glanced over. "Point taken," he said, returning himself to the temporary seating.

Aziza simply scooted herself back against the closed door, unwilling to take a second pratfall.

She looked up. "Magus … uh … Mr. Crayle, I've been given the go-ahead to read you in. On where we go next."

Here we go again, he thought. Another attractive, and no doubt deadly, female referring to him in familiar terms. "Shoot."

"Please use that word only when circumstances call for it. On the remainder of our journey." She winked. "Anyway, we've passed into Kyrgyzstan on the way to my homeland. We finish in Bukhara. My home town."

"I bet we meet up with the jet there."

"Hopefully. Or we need a Plan C."

Crayle just shook his head. Plans on top of plans. Perhaps there was a vaccine for impending insanity. He'd check with Doc Rorschach.

"Come. We'll do some breakfast in the dining car, and catch some scenery. I've already seen to the needs of your associates, Micmac and Rustom." She anticipated the raised eyebrows. "Sustenance needs." She gave that a moment. "We'll have to take special care in public spaces on the train. Small talk only. The Stans are renowned as home to every manner of spy on the planet. Even moms with little babies."

"Babies?"

"It's really the babies you have to watch. They're a distraction."

Crayle was getting used to Aziza's sense of humor. And she spoke English with a colloquial American accent. Experience implied to him an interesting backstory there.

In twenty minutes, the two sat in the dining car throwing down an ethnic smorgasbord of foods.

"The drink is popular Kyrgyz. Milk tea with salt added. The repast is Uzbek. We call it *narren*."

"I'm getting the flavors. It's mincemeat with buttermilk."

"And pepper. Here, try it with the *naan* bread."

He did. "Now that is tasty."

Aziza smiled. "For lunch, we're having more Uzbek. *Manty*."

"Which is?"

"Onions. With meat and potatoes. You'll like it."

"You must visit us someday. My wife will cook her specialty. Serrano burgers."

CHAPTER 38

Surely there would be no Hard Rock Café in Bukhara, Uzbekistan. But there it was. Crayle, Micmac, and Rustom Modi and guide, Aziza, finished their brief ride from the train station and stopped in front of it.

Aziza hopped out, leading them inside.

It looked Hard Rock, all right. It had the giant, neon-adorned Les Paul guitar out front at fully erect, welcoming all comers.

The franchisee had adorned the walls with framed, gifted guitars from such notable icons as Jimi Hendrix and Eric Clapton. Himself a musician, Micmac doubted the authenticity just a bit.

The place was packed, but everyone was either rocking out to the hard rock, engaged in conversation, or both. No one seemed to notice that two of the men carried what appeared to be rugby balls under their arms.

A quick set of juicy hamburgers and drinks later, Aziza led them to the restrooms in back. She didn't step to a door with the Ladies symbol, or point the men to Men. Instead, she activated a keypad and led them through a door adorned by a mere question mark.

In the next seconds, the faux bathroom descended below ground. Common place for the team, no one was surprised.

At the bottom there was quite a rock and roll setup. Sumptuous couches and chairs were supplemented by several large speakers perched on steel brackets, standing them out from the bright yellow walls.

"Yes, this is a STIF. We can speak freely here. Please. Have a seat," Aziza said as she punched a remote control. The speakers emanated a wandering tone that Crayle and Micmac knew would thwart any attempt at audio surveillance.

Crayle and Micmac recognized the device in her hand right away. The CIA Universal Remote. They wondered how much Jack Sommers, and more dangerous, President Stones, knew.

"Your special Smartphones will operate here," she advised. "If you require privacy, the bathroom over there," she pointed, "is safe … and doesn't go anywhere."

Crayle was first up, beating Micmac, who'd sunk deep into the sumptuous seating.

He hit a special speed dial number.

Jack Sommers picked up on the first ring.

"Where the hell—"

"Only got a minute, Jack. Fill me in. What do you know?"

Jack wanted to bite his head off. Discretion, Jack.

"Stuff going on in Iran. Previous tight relationship with Vladimir. Wanted, or thought, they were getting nuclear technology. With the Czarina, that's up in the air. She says it'd be a cold day in hell that she'll follow through with Vlad's promises."

"That's particularly good to know. But could change in a moment. It makes what we're doing even more important."

Jack caught himself again. He calmed. Some.

"What exactly—"

"Don't tell Kimbel any of this—"

The call cut off.

Crayle tried to regain the comms. No luck. He utilized the real bathroom, then stepped out.

Aziza stood just outside. With no indication that she'd listened in. Unknown to the rest, she had disestablished the phone connection.

"Comms down for a while. We need to go. We've got a flight to catch."

"We? And where to?"

"Yes, we. I'm along for the long haul."

Rustom nodded.

With that, Crayle and Micmac retrieved their rugby balls, and the eclectic strike team exfiltrated the Bukhara Hard Rock Café.

• • •

After a twenty minute ride to the airport, they found themselves standing next to a helicopter. Not the Dassault Falcon Crayle and Micmac expected.

"So what do you intend to do, Rusty?" Crayle turned to the Parsi. "Fly this thing in over Tehran, jump out here on the skids, and drop these bombs? Intel tells us their defense forces have a very good umbrella of air force fighters and missiles. Surface to air missiles. You know. SAMS from Russia."

"It's not what you think. You will appreciate my thinking far more than you can imagine. But, for now, need to know and your lack of clearance in my new spy service precludes me from reading you in."

"Rusty, I've never strangled a Parsi before. Let me see how much joy that can bring."

Aziza, at the ready behind him, applied the CIA's Dial-A-Dose set to twelve hours of restful sleep.

She'd already gotten to Micmac.

That should be plenty for where they were going next.

CHAPTER 39

It'd been Arzu's idea. She took a moment to reflect on a few thoughts she deemed important. To fill in a few missing items before Hekka left. They'd been so busy, especially at the Kizil Caves, and had travelled so far. And there might not be much time in Ürümqi for what she had to say. They found a private moment. Arzu filled in some blanks.

"The Han Chinese in Beijing declared the Xinjiang Western province a semi-autonomous region, and then spied on and controlled everything that went on there. I decided that the Muslim Uighur population needed its own spy entity. But invisible to their overlords. I named my secret and grossly unofficial creation the Free Uighur Clandestine Klub. I even considered a beneath-the-radar university in order to develop talent."

"That's quite a move considering your age at the time."

"Well, I'd heard about the Beijing Hard Rock Café being shut down by the government due to an overabundance of Mongolian prostitutes. I wasn't sure how many was just enough.

"Like the French policeman in the movie, Casablanca, 'shocked' that gambling activities were going on at *Rick's Café Américain*, the Chinese authorities were 'shocked' that sexual activities were going on at the Beijing Hard Rock. Truth be told, many developed a liking for the Mongolian working girls, as they partook in the offerings."

Hekka nodded her understanding. "We sometimes see a marked difference in people between the words and deeds."

"That was it. With a little financial backing from Hong Kong, I and my colleagues in crime opened the Hard Rock Ürümqi. It did seem a little strange for devout Muslims to front a store with alcohol and debauchery, but the Han Chinese handlers, stationed in our province's capitol, frequented the place. The godless ones considered the Muslims to be like all One God religious addicts. Hypocrites to the nth degree, they thought."

"Hypocrisy doesn't seem to be limited to any group, religious or not. Please … continue."

"Girls were lured to the task from nearby Western Mongolia and the likewise nearby 'Stans'. All conversations were recorded. A special STIF room, prepared with help from the CIA Science and Technology directorate, allowed our spies to plot and scheme freely. Little known was that undetectable CIA bugs, angled to the sky by means of the huge Les Paul guitar monument out front, which served as a reach-for-the-satellites antenna, out bound traffic only. But, in recent weeks, I've focused on your trip. So, some background on the Silk Road and Central Asia is in order. Interested?"

"I can't wait."

"There have long been Persian, Muslim, Buddhist, and Zoroastrian connections from China's Xinjiang province to the long-ago Persia. Persian traders went at least as far as Xinjiang, plying all manner of trade. Xinjiang, by the way, is the largest province in China, and the westernmost. It borders with a number of countries and has, itself, several 'Stan' ethnicities such as Kazakhs, etc. So, regarding your research, the ethnic and religious connections to the Middle East and Central, Northern, Eastern, and Southern Asia are well known and documented over a long period of time."

"Is there more?"

"Not at this time. Perhaps on the flight to the capitol. For your speech."

"Fabulous. Let's be on our way East. And let's get this done."

Hekka and Arzu were more than ready to head back to Ürümqi's Diwopu International Airport. The news media reported a major celebration that the repairs due to the previous mini-nuke attack by the Chinese insurgent, Chin Yao-wu, were now complete. Marli's landing of the Dassault Falcon 8X was destined to be the usual flawless.

With a speck of sadness that accompanies trips heading for a conclusion, Hekka and Arzu rejoined the others.

CHAPTER 40

Having bid farewell to Aziza, Hekka and her security duo, plus Arzu, flew the approximate 650 miles back to Ürümqi, where the trek through Xinjiang and its big surprises had commenced. As pilot Marli traced the landing pattern, the two passengers could see the improvements below. Yet another runway had been rebuilt from the not so long ago nuclear destruction, and entered service.

On the Falcon's flight deck, the pilot brought up a screen to display the view the other two enjoyed. "We'll be landing on that new one. Just saying."

It was obvious. A motion sensor or camera had indicated their positions in the cabin. That's how Marli knew.

"Down in fifteen. Buckle up."

Half an hour later, and past what pretended to be customs, they loaded their luggage and stepped into the same enhanced Hummer as before. How it got there, they didn't have a clue.

"Where to for my speech, Arzu? The one I'm giving as repayment for Empress Ling?"

"We're off to People's Square. Mid-town. Only place big enough!"

"Big enough? I thought perhaps a TV station. A 'no big deal' and 'low key' sort of speech."

"Actually, Ling said it needed a little publicity. Right after we finished our mission out West, a bit of advance notice went out. Anything coming from the Chinese palace gets attention here."

The trip from the airport took substantially longer than normal. They finally arrived at the park. Arzu marched Hekka to a stage, noting the jaw of her newfound spy associate had dropped. It remained in that configuration the entire way.

The Uighur took the podium.

"Ladies and gentlemen," she said in Uighur. "All 250,000 of you. I introduce to you this lovely lady from America."

The crowd was primed. It went wild. How could this one person be so important?

Hekka smiled, thanked Arzu, and took her place at the microphone. She raised both hands, palms out, to quiet the throng, only causing more uproar. Finally, the din subsided.

"People of Xinjiang. I come to you with a message from your empress in Hong Kong. I have not read it."

She unsealed an envelope she'd been guarding throughout the journey. She withdrew its contents, and read aloud.

"Xinjiang and its peoples go back thousands of years. There are Uighurs, Mongols, ethnic Chinese, Kazakhs, Tajiks, Kyrgyz, Uzbeks, Tibetans, Russians … and me."

The crowd roared. It didn't know why. It just roared.

"I am Serrano Indian. Not the India Indians with whom you are familiar, but of America. We are called indigenous. We are called Native Americans. But we are, above all, and like you, fellow human beings."

The crowd had tired of exuberance. It listened. To every word.

"Those of us throughout the Americas from the northern Arctic lands to the tip of South America … long ago … came through here."

The crowd cheered, having gotten its second breath.

"From Central Asia, and Southern Asia, my ancestors trouped eastward and northward across the land bridge linking today's Siberia to what became our state of Alaska. My research here has proven my thesis. We, the Western Hemisphere's early people ... are you!"

The crowd went wild. But, no scuffles broke out. Following Arzu's lead on the stage before them, some pressed their palms downward telling others to calm down a bit, and hear the rest.

"But enough of our linkage. Here is Empress Ling's edict. After all of your years of tribulations and work in bringing trade in both directions along the Silk Road, the new Imperial China wishes to reward you for your amalgamations of races, languages, and customs, and for making China a far better place.

"Your reward shall be freedom! As official emissary of Empress Ling, I proclaim the following." She waited a few heartbeats. "Xinjiang is now free!"

The disbelief of those present was deep and universal. After what they'd been through, it couldn't be true. Another trick by the Han Chinese to out its opponents.

Hekka continued. "Your current Semi-Autonomous Region leaders will maintain order for six months. Some will, of course, have to leave. Repatriated to the new, more concise China."

Somehow, the crowd knew. She could tell. Some of their leaders had owed obeisance to Beijing, not Xinjiang. Those would be gone.

"In six months to the day, Xinjiang will, for the first time in history, elect its own leaders. The elections will be free, and monitored."

The people throughout the park went abuzz.

"No, not monitored by Chinese, but by an independent, experienced, and unbiased crew. And to maintain the economy, the empress says that treaties between the two countries will be established, to be ratified by your first, post-SARS leaders."

Surprise registered on Hekka's face with what came next.

The entire crowd began to chant "Freedom!" over and over. Some American flags, which had become the international symbol of freedom for the masses, waved vigorously. It meant freedom from governmental tyrannies that had ravaged the so-called common people for millennia.

So this was the *little* deed, the *little* speech, Ling required as payment for Hekka's research trip. She'd gotten a Rolls-Royce for the price of a Chevy. There would be a private chat with the empress.

First, she needed to take her bow, then exit stage left.

Arzu knew. She nodded.

The crowd had turned inward, congratulating each other on the unanticipated turn of events.

"One more thing," Arzu said from the stage. "We're renaming this park. From People's Square … to Freedom Square!"

Now, those amassed went nuts. Elation atop elation.

The Uighur latched onto Hekka's arm.

"While they entertain themselves, which could last for a bit, we need to get you back to the airport. And headed home. You've done more here than I thought possible. All good. No. All wonderful. Thank you, Hekka."

She wrapped her in a serious hug.

They left. With roads near empty, they arrived at the airport in record time. Marli was wheels up in twenty.

Arzu waved as the plane soared into the heavens. She could feel it. She had a brand new and indelible friendship.

And a country.

• • •

The flight back to Hong Kong took a little less time with prevailing tailwinds than the other way. All aboard rested well and arrived several hours later at Hong Kong International. Ling's limo immediately swept them off to the palace atop Victoria Peak.

Phoebe and Lenny were shown to a special room where they could utilize their Smartphones freely, watch television, and enjoy some snacks. They'd join their leader and the empress later.

• • •

Hekka had a moment to herself. She remembered well how this whole trip had kicked off, starting in Hong Kong. She put on her AI headset, and saw it all again. It seemed so real.

Hekka and Ling had taken seats opposite each other in the dining room. The room itself did nothing to dispel the aura of the splendiferous original Ch'in period. China's first emperor would have been quite comfortable in this setting.

When the servers finished providing the typical repast for this day of the week, they bowed as they backed from the presence of the empress. When Yellow daughter, their supervisor in the current task, followed suit, the two spoke unencumbered by witnesses.

"Ling, I owe you more than I can say for your help with my quest. I will try to avoid overdoing my expressions of gratitude."

"We have both achieved much from humble beginnings. I would love to travel to America to have you show me the lands of your heritage, as you will see mine."

"You are known the world over, Ling. Empress of China. I haven't quite made it that far. It would take some heavy-duty disguising to keep the press and curiosity seekers unaware."

"But your position, and that of Magus as Director of Central Intelligence, could provide all the hidden identity I would require. Not true?"

Hekka just smiled. She reasoned that spies rarely were requested to provide their expertise to foreign heads of state.

"I have only one minor request."

"At this point, I'm supposed to say, *Aha!* We can skip that. You are giving me so much assistance. I would be happy to grant your request, Ling. What is it?"

Ling told her.

Hekka reacted by turning catatonic. She barely breathed.

"You will fly from Hong Kong to Ürümqi," Ling had said. "It is the capitol of the northwestern most province, Xinjiang. There, you will give a prepared speech to the local people who assemble. Yellow will help me with the publicity."

"A speech? To a crowd? Ling, my dear friend …"

She stopped. Hekka knew that, most of all, imperial palace walls had ears. Big ears. She mouthed, "I'm a spy."

"And …"

"Number One rule: Don't get noticed. Number Two rule: If noticed, don't be remembered. Giving speeches to crowds is not in the manual, as Magus would say."

"I understand. But, you promised. And you need the help I've offered."

"You're right. And we Serrano are honorable, if nothing else. Well … wait … what is the language of these people? Surely it's not English."

"You are familiar with a Doctor Rorschach?"

She knew, Hekka surmised. "Wouldn't it be better if you gave the speech in person? Cement your relationship with those far away peoples?"

"Okay. It's not that heavy of a speech. So you need to stay here and keep China running. I get it."

"Do you?"

"What could this speech possibly confer? That you'll be shipping them some of this wonderful Kung Pao Beef and Moo Shoo Pork?"

"It's more than that. More important."

"What, then?"

"You simply inform those good people of my Xinjiang Independence Plan."

Hekka sat back. Her eyes wide open. Her forehead tightly stretched.

"Yes, my dear. The Uighurs are getting their freedom. Their own country."

There. The simulation concluded. During their real-life conversation, Ling had never mentioned independence for the Uighurs. For Xinjiang.

At that point, Hekka decided one thing for sure. Micmac's new AI project was here and now pronounced DOA. Dead. On. Arrival.

CHAPTER 41

Crayle'd heard no more about the sex slaves spies from Pakistan. The ones who dove overboard and swam beneath the pier in Rustom's first aborted incursion attempt at Iran's southeasternmost port. That was behind them. Spy philosophy always required one to assess the current state of affairs, then move forward.

To that end, Crayle recalled requiring Rustom to have his own spy network in place for the operation. The Parsi took that to heart and even came up with names such as Operation Overthrow or Operation Cyrus or Operation Darius to show his seriousness regarding the effort. So far, there'd been little sharing on the subject of this spy network. Perhaps the Parsi had taken the notion of compartmentalization too seriously. Or Crayle had become necessarily nosy.

• • •

While Crayle waxed pensive, many miles distant four Pakistani females arrived at Tehran's Presidential Palace. Completely attired in black burkas, they were recognizable to no one. And, not as a side benefit, defeated any attempts by the facial recognition software so popular in the far less religiously strict West.

Still, the women were herded into a room by their slave traders. These were the same men who'd taken charge of them at the southeast Iranian port of Bandar Beheshti. The burkas now each sported a two-inch square number in red ink such that, once sampled, the women could be best allocated to the ultimate sex slave owner. That could include Iran's leader.

Two men sat in an outer room and joked about their slaves, who might be secretly swapping outfits, or numbers, just to confound things.

What was unknown to them was that these were not sex slaves at all. They were the spy operatives of one Rustom Modi. Each was a Zoroastrian by religion and traced her heritage back to ancient Persia. At that time, their belief system ruled, as opposed to the era of persecution brought on by the Arab conquest.

While the less senior of the two busied himself chewing on hashish, the other spoke.

"The women inside, I am told, are special."

The other, already into a stupor, babbled a response.

"Then we should see why they are special."

"Not for us. They are the best of their Pakistani lot. Designated for the highest officials."

"But the highest officials are the Ayatollahs. Not just any Ayatollahs. The Grand Ayatollahs. There are five of them."

"That is so. If it is we who spoil them, we shall receive the most severe of punishments here on Earth. Only the One God would exact a more harsh ending. For any human being."

"Then we must protect these women. I shall enter their room to see that they are well and comfortable."

"To do that, they must remove their burkas. In private, of course, so you can report back to higher ups that they have been personally inspected. To ensure quality has been maintained."

"And that no future claims of harm can be brought to our doorstep."

With that, and an affirmative nod from his associate, the guard unlocked the door and stepped inside.

Before he could say a word, one of the so-called sex slaves removed her black burka head covering.

He stopped cold. Clearly, he saw before him the most beautiful woman he could imagine.

She handed her hood to another, and stepped around him.

He motioned for her to remove the remaining garment.

In the next seconds, the other woman rolled and twisted the head covering into a garrote.

She applied it with extreme prejudice.

The third spy yanked off her own covering, clasping it over the guard's mouth.

There came no outcries. No sounds at all.

Outside, the other guard started to worry. His cohort had been inside for several minutes. If that man allowed his lust to outweigh his need for survival, it would be both of them who'd suffer a horrific terminal fate.

After quickly checking hallways and seeing no potential witnesses, he entered the room.

What the second guard saw prompted him to reach for his weapon.

The third of the 'sex slaves' was disrobing. She yanked her burka completely free.

But, she wasn't a she.

The man of the same height as the others wore standard Iranian male street dress.

He ditched his burka in back, under his shirt.

The other three acted in concert, as they had with the first guard.

In seconds, the second guard lay dead on the floor.

Quickly, the first two spies re-donned their head coverings. The man led them from the room.

It was soon clear his role was as the requisite male, escorting the women into public spaces. As required by the religious authorities.

They'd succeeded thus far. They'd made it from Pakistan to Iran. To the Presidential Palace.

The man had the layout memorized. He led them to the suite of the country's leader. Grand Ayatollah Number One.

Guards along the way expected four sex slaves, and asked where was the fourth.

The man, in perfect Farsi, bemoaned that she'd taken ill. A virus of some sort.

The Iranian leader's guard rapped at the door. He entered and told the Grand Ayatollah the sex slaves had arrived.

Grand Ayatollah Jahni was against sex slavery. For any reason. Men, he'd learned at his mother's knee, were to be protectors, especially of women. He only took them in, but never partook. He assured they would be as pure when they left, as when they'd entered.

He dismissed the guard.

"Please. Be comfortable on the sofa. You are safe here. You shall not be molested while in my care."

There was an old saw in the Middle East that, if a woman was denied relations by a male, she was therefore unattractive. That the One God had created her so.

"May I speak?" asked the main spy.

"Please."

"Someone gave me a paper. To read. Then, destroy. I did. They are words for you, and you alone."

"My room here in the palace is bug free. In all manners. Tell me the message."

"There is to be a Grand Hajj. Everyone will go. From Tehran to Mecca. Each man, woman, and child shall be allocated $1,000, in U.S. currency, to make the journey. But it must be taken this week."

"But, why this week? And why pay them?"

"Each person, who can financially and otherwise go, is required by our religion to make this pilgrimage at least once. The financial amount assures all can fulfill this requirement."

"Again, why is this being done?"

"Because your predecessor came within a few miles of detonating a nuclear device, an air burst, intended to destroy our holiest site. For eternity."

"Yes. And blame it on the Israelis."

"As it turned out, a Jewish man from America saved Mecca."

CHAPTER 42

The rumors were out. But unverified. Tehran residents would soon be commanded to affect a mass exodus, each with a government supplied stipend, to Hajj to Mecca. For men, women, and children. And with all expenses paid, as well.

For equity in the process, Christians, Jews, and Zoroastrians—known in short form as Zoros—would substitute destinations relevant to their particular beliefs. What wasn't in the public discourse was that the latter would arrive just in time for a speech by Rustom Modi and Grand Ayatollah Jahni.

• • •

The Grand Ayatollah responded to the Pakistani spy's latest remark.

"Yes. One Lenny Lipschitz, our intelligence discovered."

"The whole scheme brought to the front the vulnerability of Mecca to lunatics with nuclear weapons. The time is now to see to this Grand Hajj. And, I mean, now!"

"It makes perfect sense to me. Is there a catch?"

"Each one who accomplishes this shall receive an additional $1,000 upon return to Tehran."

"Just Tehran? May I assume that this will extend to the remainder of our country?"

"Yes. You can. And to be fair, non-Muslims shall receive the same deal for a pilgrimage to their most religious site. The Christians and Jews to Jerusalem. Zoroastrians to Persepolis. And so forth."

"A great deal of money is involved. Before I announce such a thing, I must be assured it will be there."

"There is a guarantee."

"A guarantee? By whom?"

The man handed him a slip of paper.

Grand Ayatollah Jahni blanched. Then, read. "Kimbel Stones."

While the male 'sex slave' reassumed his burka disguise, the other three escorted Jahni out the door onto the balcony.

To the cleric's total surprise, the square below was jammed with thousands. The crowd's raucous banter ceased the moment their leader stepped into view.

Jahni truly expected the choruses of 'Death To America' that his government, and those preceding, had paid good money to suborn.

But, no. Just an awesome silence.

He stood a few feet back from the balcony wall, mostly due to a lifelong fear of heights. He glanced down. Two of the slave spies were seated facing him, holding the sides of a story board tablet. With his speech writ large.

Thank God, he thought. This was no time for impromptu. Each word had to be correct. Jahni held his hands high as if to silence the quiescent throng. Not necessary. Just habit.

He began.

"Blessings to all from the One God. I deliver my speech to you in English so the Western media cannot get it wrong."

The crowd laughed. They felt the referenced media did not get Iranian speeches wrong by accident.

"This is a special moment for me. I've devoted my life to the One God. Allah. The spirit of the Holy Qur'an tells, and has told us for centuries, those who can make the Hajj to Mecca, must do so. At least once per lifetime."

Yes, they knew that.

"Unfortunately, those without the means could not make the journey. My countrymen, I stand before you with a new pledge. From me. Your leader. I promise $1,000 US Dollar equivalent in our currency. Up front. When your Hajj is complete, another stipend of equal amount shall be received. By you."

The bulk of the crowd could not believe their ears. No less than the Grand Ayatollah Jahni just underwrote the fulfillment of a dream for the faithful. His word was good. He'd never let them down in the past.

A gargantuan cheer erupted.

Jahni let it run for a couple of minutes, then raised his hands.

Silence.

"You shall contact this website." He provided the Holy URL. "... and you shall arrange receipt of the payment amount. There is, as the Americans say, a catch. You must leave within the next three days.

Consternation slammed the crowd like a huge wave.

"Not to worry. Transportation, lodging, food, and medical needs shall be provided. And though we've had issues in the past—we tried to blow up their oil fields—the Saudi government is fully on board. Oh, and none of the expenses of travel, other than for souvenirs, shall be charged to either payment. My treat."

Jahni smiled broadly. They were taking this news exceptionally well.

"You shall finish your Hajj and have $2,000 US equivalent to spend as you desire. You could be inspired by your visit to this holiest place. And, it is important to add, anyone trying to take your stipends from you or interfere with your pilgrimage, shall be apprehended and charged with Holy crimes against the One God."

The crowd generated another uproarious cheer.

Don't get in the way of public support, someone wise had told him. It could have been that Magus Crayle. At the B Summit. He'd thank him some day.

"Now, go in peace. Make your plans swiftly. Employers are hereby ordered to accommodate this momentous sojourn."

The deeply religious Jahni was impassioned by the text he'd just read. The spy team could tell, he was about to go off script. Historically, a political success could turn into a nightmare in a sentence or two.

The two spies holding the Jahni-prompter vigorously pointed at the final page.

"Oh, and those not Muslim? The same Holy pilgrimage is offered. Christians and Jews to Jerusalem. Zoroastrians to Persepolis. And similar for others. When the Hajj is complete for Tehran, I shall initiate the same for those outside of the capitol. So, go. Iran shall lead the way. To Holy harmony, and to a peace the likes of which the world has never seen."

CHAPTER 43

As the din in the Presidential Palace square below faded, the five on the balcony heard knocking on the outer door. It increased in intensity followed by the addition of rifle butts being applied with brute force.

Jahni checked his Holy Smartphone.

"It's the others! The other four Grand Ayatollahs … and their personal guard forces!"

"Of course," spy number one observed. "You are destroying their game of greed for power and wealth. The one they've been playing for years."

"Then, consider the real reason they killed my predecessor! His abortive nuclear attack on Mecca would not just destroy our religious center, but ruin their deals!"

"We're outta here, Your Holiness. Or whatever." Spy two spoke into the microphone hidden in her burka hood, "Exfil! Now!"

In short order, an arctic white helicopter, sporting a star and crescent livery as well as the world-recognized red cross of the eponymous agency, appeared.

It hovered thirty feet above the balcony.

A narrow rope ladder fell from an open door.

Jahni jumped back.

The others grabbed him, jerking him to the swinging ladder.

Spy three affixed him with what appeared to be double zip tie FlexiCuffs.

"We have to leave. They'll kill us all!" said adrenaline infused spy one.

"I can't climb up with these!" Jahni nodded at his restraints.

"Not to worry."

The four sex slave spies similarly attached themselves.

No one could fall.

Up went the chopper.

Then, off at full tilt to the southwest.

Most of the crowd attempted to rush away from the square. Each wanting to be among the first to sign up for the Grand Hajj.

Only a few of them turned at the sound of the helicopter. And saw their religious and political leader, plus four burka-clad others, being hoisted aloft. Dangling like literary participles.

They all thought the same thought.

The One God absolutely did work in mysterious ways.

• • •

They'd transited a good ten miles when the hyperventilating, terrified Grand Ayatollah saw motion above him.

Up at the top of the swinging pendulum of a ladder. A man clad in black.

That the person climbing down toward him needed both hands for a grip did not hide the pair of wire clippers clamped in his jaw.

The Grand Ayatollah's mind nearly snapped. He'd made the speech, but the logistics of the religious treks had clearly been set up without his knowledge. He was no longer necessary.

They'd cut him loose. To fall to Earth.

He was now beyond terrified.

The terror was short lived.

The pilot hovered, then descended the aircraft until all five pairs of feet touched ground.

The black-clad operative clipped all wrists free, then scampered back up the ladder. He pulled it up behind him, and signaled thumbs up to the copilot.

He took a seat as the chopper moved off to one side, then landed.

All helped their charge, Grand Ayatollah and leader of Iran, into the helicopter.

Two spies took seats to either side and clasped his hands to calm and comfort him. For now. For the flight ahead.

The chopper lifted off, reasserting its former flight path southwest.

The third sex slave retrieved a crystal cylinder from beneath her disguise. Courtesy of the American CIA, she loaded Jahni with a six-hour dose. He slept a peaceful sleep.

CHAPTER 44

There they were. The Pope, his personal Cardinal Richelieu, and a host of others. Not in the Vatican where one would expect to find them, but rather at the pontiff's favorite fishing hole at a lake northeast of Rome. It was the Cardinal who had, or thought he had, the dominant sense of humor.

"If the Pope can pray to catch a fish, and does it, what chance do the rest of us have?"

While the others chuckled, the holiest Roman Catholic appeared consumed with serious thought, unrelated to the sport at hand. The Cardinal picked up on his boss' prevailing mood.

"I can see by your expression, that encounter with the Muslim and Jewish religious leaders in Casablanca has smitten your heart."

The Pope nodded. "The American made them eat pork."

"But they were Muslims and Jews. How …"

"He just got them to fast, promising a monumental meal."

"But they would just refuse. They, devout as they were, would just go hungry."

"True. All he needed was one to break. He counted on it.'

"It was the Jew, wasn't it? Israel's top cleric."

"Yes. Bacon has a special aroma when it's hot. It wafts through the air like a demon, invading the body and spirit through the sense of smell. We mustn't forget, though, the top Jewish cleric possesses a high IQ and street sense as well. Similar to that of the American president."

"I see. You imply, Your Eminence, that the two were in league, so to speak."

"It crossed my mind. And when he ate and emoted the gasps of joy, the others said, in effect, oh hell, and dove in. We clerics have learned over the years that, if you're going to sin, go all in." The Pope chuckled at his humorous rhyme.

Seeing that it was okay, the others joined in. A notable parallel to the acts during that special recent session in Casablanca.

"The three religions accede to One God. The Creator. One God. Three religions. Mr. Crayle, who ran the session posed the monumental question. What could happen among humanity to make Him smile?"

The cardinals thought.

The one from Saint Louis, the Missouri Saint Louis, raised his hand.

The Pope nodded his way.

"It is clear to all that we can't kill our way to peace. It's been tried. Humanity is regularly punished for not choosing the obvious."

While the Pope appreciated the accurate observation, he couldn't allow the young cleric to steal his thunder. "The answer to all, and for eternity, reduces to two words. World Peace."

"It's never been achieved. Not even close!"

The Pope achieved apogee. He offered them the tease.

"Magus Crayle, when he gathered the Middle Eastern top clerics, gave us the answer."

There were several quick glances exchanged among the cardinals. They appeared as famished birds, checking to see which one had the worm.

All eyes snapped back to the Pope.

The answer was unanimous.

"Bacon!"

Finally done, and back at their shore-side cottage, the cardinal stripped down to his underwear. He stepped before a full-length mirror, and beamed at his reflection. A t-shirt covered his torso. It sported A bat. A ball. A bird.

And lettering.

The **Saint Louis Cardinals** in bold.

CHAPTER 45

A special session of the Senate Intel Committee had been called. National Defense stood at extreme risk, it was said. Of course, overstating the situation facing the country was so not new that comparisons with 'boy cries wolf' were even boring. The players could still put on a proper act. As one did now.

Mavis McNary, the ranking member at the Senate confirmation hearing, was livid. "We need to have the candidate for Director of Central Intelligence here in person to pose our questions, Mister Chairman!"

"He's virtual and disguised for reasons of National Security."

"This is insane!"

Already ramped up to viciously dismember whatsoever candidate President Kimbel Stones' party offered, she dropped forward, both palms slapping the surface of her podium. Gasping for breath.

"We'll take five minutes," said the chairman.

Two nearby members of her party helped the senator to her seat.

"She needs privacy," said her party whip.

Her number one, the party's Senate whip, escorted McNary into a small uncomfortable room.

A man she recognized only too well as Senator Duncan of the opposition followed them, shut and locked the door behind him.

"What? Hey, Senator Whatsisface. This is private! Shoo!"

"It's okay," said the whip. "I've been meaning to tell you. He's with us."

Her countenance fell into supreme quandary mode.

"Credibility," her arch enemy said.

"And why? What motivates you to our side?"

"Money, ideology, and power are your choices."

"Look. I … we have an Executive Branch entity telling us what we get to see and hear! They can't do that! It's … uh … unconstitutional! If it isn't, it needs to be!"

"You already know the answer. You didn't achieve your level of success without it. Senator McNary, pick your battles. Don't know who said that, but someone also said the CIA types can hurt you six ways to sundown. Let it go."

She didn't have to think long. Swamp creatures like her needed to be strong, and careful. A long deep breath, and out, relaxed her.

"Okay. We'll do it. I'll come up with some indelible conditions they can just ignore. We'll both win."

"As I knew it would be, there's wisdom in your words. I'm feeling a run for the presidency the very next opportunity."

"Hey. I'm seasoned, connected, and sneaky enough to get in. And, whoa! I can get my revenge from the catbird seat."

Before he could move, she planted a big kiss, then left the room with her whip. Back into the committee chambers.

The door closed. The opposition senator made a call on his very special Smartphone. To Langley.

"Done," was the sole word used.

The five minutes passed, and the senator had recovered her composure. And launched back into attack mode.

The chairman pre-empted her. "Your time has expired, Madam Senator."

"You said that … you said Madam … as if I'm the head of a group of whores!"

"I rest my case, Madam Senator. Next."

• • •

Finally, the Senate got the purpose of their hearing underway. A pixilated visage showed on the large flat screen monitor. The voice, disguised.

The chairman directed his attention to the screen. "We are set up and ready to calibrate the voice stress analysis lie detection app. Are you ready?"

What sounded like *Yes* emanated from the speakers. On the other end, candidate Magus Crayle intended to have some virtual fun with this.

"Mr. Candidate, do you intend to tell the truth?"

"No, Senator. I intend to lie."

The technician present, who loomed over a laptop, glanced up at the chairman. "He failed on the voice stress. It means he intends to tell the truth."

While the chairman was as loyal to his party as they get, it was not easy to swallow the admonition he had in mind for the candidate. Instead, he provided the conclusion for all the question mark faces in the audience.

"So, that he intends to lie is a lie." He pounded the gavel. "In this chamber, two lies make a truth. We are good to go."

CHAPTER 46

Mavis McNary sat in the catbird seat. As U.S. Senate Intelligence Committee ranking member, it fell to her to take the lead in vetting any and all candidates for Director of Central Intelligence. As was common in Congress, and especially its upper chamber, that position denoted substantial authority and power.

With the session proclaimed open, and having dispensed with the preliminaries, she posed her first question to the pixilated big screen provided for the purpose by the CIA's Science and Technology Directorate. "What was your first security clearance?"

The image responded in a processed but comprehensible voice. "I was informed by the sole other person in the room that my security clearance was so high, it would be illegal to even discuss it."

She glanced at the CIA technician in charge, who confirmed existence of such a lofty level.

"So you, or those like you, were involved with the so-called mini-nuke weapons detonated here and there around the world."

"As DCI candidate, I have been fully briefed, Senator."

"And of what manner of briefs do we speak?"

"Calvin Klein, Your Honor. Black."

That response brought laughs all around.

Lenny, back from Asia and a questionable invite to a monumental event such as this, slapped his knee. To the extent it sounded like a gunshot.

The senator, and others, ducked in reaction.

Then, realizing the absence of any material threat, the Chairman yelled, "Order!" Followed by a pounding of the precious gavel.

McNary straightened in her chair. "Any threat to any senator is a serious, no … severe, crime, Mr. Candidate!"

She clamped her jaw to let the mouth muscles indicate the degree of her adamancy.

"Oh, I wouldn't commit physical violence against you, Senator." He paused. "Not personally." The pixilation dutifully disguised the candidate's smile.

"Your type sports a unique sense of humor. I'll leave it at that."

As if on purpose, the premier senator from the other party passed gas. Loud enough for all to hear.

Uproarious laughter was followed by the ensuing, unanimous applause.

McNary was furious.

"Senator Duncan! If you don't cease and desist, I shall have to re-establish decorum … by placing you out in the hall."

The offending politician crossed his arms, but withheld a response.

"All right," said the Chairman. "Potty break time. Back in fifteen."

"Clunk!"

• • •

Overseas, Crayle was mentally finished with boots on the ground operations. Just a couple more things to do. Those completed, he'd head back home to install himself on Langley's vaunted seventh floor. He needed to cut loose his former invisible ties to the Company, a euphemism for America's CIA, and make them org-chart solid. It was time to go public. First order of business, inform pain-in-the-neck Senator McNary that he was indeed the voice-disguised, pixilated DCI candidate image she'd seen during the so-called senate confirmation hearing.

He needed to put a real face and name to the title. After careful consideration, he decided to have a Stones' party senator, not the chairman, have an underling inform her. That low level approach could knock her down a notch. But Crayle knew how Washington, D.C. worked. Not worked. Operated.

He called her direct personal number, obtained through the president's old friends and former colleagues at the NSA.

• • •

Soon after the surprise, and heart ramping call, Senator Mavis McNary exited the one person bathroom, wondering how the hell the candidate knew she was alone … and there. Her phone vibrated. Potty break over. In short order, she was back in the chamber, and addressed the Senate Confirmation assembly.

She merely utilized the precise words just provided her by the mystery candidate. Excluding his name.

The throng fell into an immediate hush. A noisy hush.

The Chairman brought order with a pound of his gavel.

"By proclamation," he began. Scanning the crowd with his most intense look.

"All for confirming candidate John Doe as Director of Central Intelligence, say aye."

They did.

"Opposed."

Silence.

No one could appose the worldwide peace in the offing as McNary had elucidated.

The gavel pounded once more.

McNary smiled at her colleagues. She'd just demonstrated leadership, and had not felt so right about something for a long, long time.

The Chairman was not quite finished.

"Session adjourned," got it done.

CHAPTER 47

The nuclear strike team consisting of Crayle, Micmac, Rustom, Aziza, and the MI-6 Apostles boarded the special ops Dhow in Turkmenistan. Those who'd been encouraged to sleep on the way from Bukhara, were rousing. Within a few minutes, Rustom was nowhere in sight.

And there was someone else on board. The one who Crayle'd wrote of as a figment of his imagination. The one called Nattie. His jaw dropped when he saw her. He shook his head in disbelief, and moved on.

He made the first observation. "We can feel the movement of the boat. We're at sea somewhere."

Micmac supplied the sailor view. "Not too much movement. Likely a bay. Or inland. A lake." He nodded. "Check out that chart over there."

Nattie, a little wobbly with the motion, stepped carefully to a navigator's table. She examined the map.

"Is there writing on it?" Micmac asked. "It would be in pencil."

"Yes. The printing says, Caspian Sea. There's a pencil line from the right. From a port named Turkmenbashi. The line goes left, toward Baku on the West side. But it turns South right in the middle."

She stepped back.

"What is it?"

"The line … it goes South. Due South."

"And …"

Nattie brought the chart for him to see.

"Oh. It goes down to the southern shore."

Crayle couldn't see the map from his position. "They must intend to take the bomb off there. From there, transport it to the capitol. To Tehran."

"They don't need us for that," Micmac observed. "What happens to us?"

No response. No one knew.

Micmac remained focused. "The line is continuous. Due South, over the shore area, and to Tehran."

Crayle had it. "Of course. When I was on this same specially equipped Dhow, we sailed from the Emirates to Das Island, out in the Gulf. When we arrived, they …"

"It's amphibious!" Micmac made the obvious deduction.

"So, what then in Tehran? Park the boat at the government buildings, and get a safe distance away?"

"Back to what happens to us?"

"Yeah. Does Rusty have us going down with the ship?"

"We don't know. He could blame America except the nukes wouldn't leave any evidence."

Nattie returned the chart to its table. She saw a remote control, and pressed POWER.

A very bright LED flat screen popped on, providing an under water view.

She used the controls to move the camera providing the visual. She hit PAUSE.

"Oh!"

Smack on the centerline of the keel, something else they hadn't counted on. A submersible. With enough room for a human.

Nattie zoomed in.

"Oh, my!"

One of the nuclear rugby balls was attached.

Crayle made the deduction this time into the hush of his fellow prisoners.

"Here are the likely possibilities. One. Rustom uses the submersible to deliver a bomb. It's not amphibious, so that doesn't get it to the capitol. Two. He escaped somewhere back there, leaving the other bomb on the Dhow. Then, remote controls it, and us, to Tehran."

The next option, Three, was interrupted as the hatch swung open, and Rustom entered.

"How did you get loose?" He stepped to Nattie, grabbing her by the arm.

She pushed back with her free hand. "I'm on your side, now, Rustom." She smiled, deploying her Pattie-clone dimples. "You must be lonely. With your wife in Portugal. I can fix that."

He turned to his Apostles first mate, standing behind. "Take her to my cabin. Tie her down good."

"Ooh. Tie me up. Wife been gone long?"

"You need to be isolated. You're a danger to me."

He was right. He just didn't know how dangerous.

Within a few seconds, they were gone.

As Rustom launched into a diatribe of how his needs and goals superseded the lives and liberties of his guests, their head snapped from him to the flat screen.

He turned.

There, replete in scuba gear, was a diminutive individual entering the submersible.

Before Rustom could act, Nattie launched herself and the craft. She turned to wave as she motored away from the Dhow at full speed.

His first notion was to give chase. Yet, pursuing someone of questionable sanity and who possessed a nuclear bomb, no matter how small, seemed a fool's errand if there ever was one.

Fifteen minutes later, the bomb detonated.

Having been installed on the submersible with This Side Toward Enemy facing forward, the majority of its force pushed in that direction. It slung the entire southern third of the Caspian Sea at the distant seashore.

While the peripheral effect was minimized by the directionality of the device, heavy waves buffeted Baku, and violently shook the Dhow.

Knocked to the floor, an adrenalin-stoked Rustom Modi jumped to his feet, grabbed a letter opener knife from the navigator's desk and, one-by-one, cut the Crayle team's ties.

"Plan C, Mr. Crayle!"

• • •

Propelled up the slope of the sea bed at the Caspian Sea's South end, the quantum of water leaped into the air in a spectacular sight.

Those within a twenty mile radius had, at first, transfixed on the explosion. Now, they ran. Full bore.

Frequently, they cast quick glances behind. Awestruck at the gargantuan wave flying perhaps fifty feet above the beaches.

Completing the arc, the huge mass of liquid splashed down, as if aimed, on Tehran's government district.

• • •

Modi had switched from the hull to the mast camera to provide the view they had of the mayhem.

"That didn't happen," Crayle muttered.

"Basic hydrodynamics," said Micmac. "Nattie did that. She died saving us."

Crayle's next epiphany came easily. "Nattie didn't just show up. Rusty brought her here. He put her in with us as a spy. The restraints on her as well was the sales pitch. So we'd speak freely."

Micmac picked up his thinking. "So, she had some hidden means to cut her bindings. He just didn't expect her to turn double agent, and help us."

"In a way, she kind of made up for her psychotic twin, Pattie."

The former Navy SEAL nodded. "Who knows? If we get out of this mess, maybe there's a star for Nattie at Langley."

CHAPTER 48

Micmac had his hands firmly on the wheel. "Mag! That bomb was directional. How much force are we dealing with?"

"About 95% pushing the water toward Tehran. The rest, sideways and back at us."

Even though most of the bomb's force was directed away from them, the remaining 5% of a miniaturized nuclear device mercilessly pummeled the Dhow carrying Crayle, Micmac, Aziza, Rustom Modi, and the Apostles. The severe creaking of the wooden structure portended the bindings coming undone … in a second or two.

Hanging onto the navigation table with both arms, Crayle and Micmac needed an out.

"Straight ahead, the mid-southern end of the Caspian. The opening for Lalumière's cooling water tunnel."

"It heads due South. To the center of the country. Of Iran. Where they tried to create a bomb from the one China supplied."

"All gone when the Frenchman detonated that one."

"But this map, left behind by Nattie, indicates …"

"Wait! Scan the deck!"

Crayle operated the mast camera's toggle.

"They're gone! The Apostles! Gone!"

"But they're running the boat!"

"Not any more!"

A catching of breaths.

"Okay. I, Captain Micmac, just promoted you from team leader to First Mate."

"Aye, Cap'n."

Crayle held onto the heavy brass tubes put in place for rough seas. He scanned the board full of knobs and switches with squiggle labels beneath each.

"It's Arabic," Aziza interpreted Crayle's mystified countenance. She fairly jumped from the bench seat to his side. "What's this? It says REEF."

Former sailor, Micmac, knew.

"It furls the sails. Press it!"

She did as ordered.

The camera system, fed by the key press, rotated to show the sails de-deploying onto their rotating spars.

"Next?"

"Find something to move the masts out of the way."

They took a heavy roll to port.

Aziza lost her one-hand hold. Her body, about to cast her head first into the hull, and knock her unconscious or worse, was saved by a quick left hand grab from Crayle.

With all his strength, he pulled her back to station.

She recovered her hand hold just as the Dhow righted again.

She scanned the panel. "Here it is!"

"Hit it!"

She did.

Eyes darted to the screen.

The masts now with all sails furled, rotated aft on their base hinges. An automatic feature secured them to the deck.

Aziza and the other two held on for a major rise, then dip as extreme currents rebounded against the boundaries of the Caspian.

"Next?"

"Batten hatches!"

"Batten? I don't know that word in Arabic."

"Means fasten. Lock tight."

She found the button to make their compartment waterproof, and pressed it. "Next?"

"Find DIVE on the panel. Take 'er down. To sixty feet."

Crayle, the mathematician, converted as if on autopilot.

"18.46 meters."

"18.46 meters, aye," Aziza confirmed.

The sophisticated Dhow systems took her to depth smoothly, given the ambient, competing sea currents. Driven by the detonation of the bomb.

A *WHOOSH* from behind goosed the Dhow forward as a long wave rebound from the Sea's North shore caught up with them.

A boat's steering is served primarily from the rudder, hinged at its front aspect. Its movement could swing a boat starboard or larboard, depending on the input of the helmsman at the wheel. Designers anticipated sail or motor propulsion to push the craft ahead, not under the current situation. They were being shoved fifty feet to the right of the tunnel's opening.

Micmac fought the wheel.

He was losing.

In seconds they'd smash against the rapidly inclining seabed. To be turned into splintered wood and flesh.

Obliterated.

Aziza yelled. "Next?"

"Side thrusters! Starboard side!"

Little time left.

"Here!" she yelled as she slammed her palm down on the button.

As advertized, starboard side thrusters shoved them left.

There!

Into the mouth of Lalumière's tunnel they surged.

The tunnel served to eliminate the whipping currents that battered the Dhow. Its automated sonar anti-collision system jumped into action, operating the side thrusters and integrated ballasting system to keep them centered, and away from the rough-hewn walls.

The Dhow settled.

Crayle retook his seat on the bench. The visual on the forward bulkhead spurred a notion. He stared down at the deck, and recalled the giant, German mining device recently used to drill a navigable water tunnel across and under the Iberian Peninsula. The Aryan Alliance. This was their specialty. And what if the former Portuguese nemesis, Martim, had paid them in full, with one of the three mini-nukes he possessed. Two had exploded under water just East of the Pillars of Hercules, effectively the starting guns for President Stones' boat race. That took the team to Casablanca. And the B Summit.

He looked up.

With the Dhow on autopilot, Micmac and Aziza took seats to his left and right.

Without a thought, he wrapped an arm around them, and gave a tug.

They responded in kind.

"Well, team," he said. "We need a map of the tunnel system. We know there's no room to turn around. If we stop, and throw it in reverse, all hell breaks loose when we emerge from the tunnel."

Aziza spoke. "Mag, if I may." She pulled free the tethers that had secured her purse. "Nattie gave me this. For you. I thought I could tell from her look, we wouldn't see her again." She handed Crayle a brown, heavy paper envelope. With a dark red wax seal.

He opened it, and read aloud.

"When you read this, I'll be gone. Knowing what my twin sister did, I needed to make things right. A little back story. My adoptive mother, Anastasia of Romanov lineage, took me in. She russianized my name. Natalie to Natalya. My nickname, Nattie, still worked. I spent the years after adoption in Saint Petersburg. When the bomb went off in Monte Carlo, at the end of the Grand Prix, it wiped out my birth father, the Prince. I never got to know either him or my mother. Anastasia became Mom.

"Anyway, if successful, my action with the submersible and the directional bomb aimed forward at Tehran, should put the damper, in both meanings, on those who govern there."

Before they could process fully what they'd just heard, an oblivious Rustom Modi, now well enough to walk, exited the Captain's Cabin, papers in hand.

"I found the plans!"

Aziza jumped up. She guided him by the arm to a seat. "Rustom, you're better?"

Seated, he appeared fully in control.

"Yes. The stability now gives me peace. But, look. I heard your words. There's a listening system in the captain's quarters. I found this map." He handed it to Crayle.

The other three scanned it from the sides. And realized what it was.

"It's the Lalumière water system. Designed by the French company he worked for. It's not just a single North-South run. It branches out."

Micmac got it. "So, Mag, the Grand Ayatollah leaders justified the system as subterranean irrigation. Almost a blessing in this part of the world."

Aziza picked it up. "That was a specialty in Central Asia for hundreds, maybe thousands of years. Especially in Xinjiang. To avoid evaporation from the unceasing desert heat. Of mountain and glacier runoff."

"Look," Micmac pointed at the map. "The main artery heads South to Fasd, where the bomb factory was being put together."

The Parsi pointed. "A branch heads southwest. To a reservoir."

"Is that good, Rustom?"

"It's the reservoir of Persepolis. Capital of ancient Persia."

He drew a slow breath.

"Home."

"Mr. Micmac," Crayle took command. "Set a course in the ship's computer for branching right at the appropriate time."

"Uh, a Dhow is a boat, not a ship, Cap'n."

Crayle produced a Captain Queeg grin.

Micmac, with serious help from Aziza, punched in the requisite data, then sat back. To finally relax.

CHAPTER 49

They made it. The Dhow containing Crayle, Micmac, Rustom, and Aziza pushed into a large reservoir in southwest Iran. The man who'd originated and led the mission, Rustom Modi, showed the others to quarters.

"The food here is excellent. Please rest. I have something to attend to." He whispered something into Crayle's ear, and was gone. Elsewhere in the facility, he met up with the team of Pakistani spies that'd confiscated the Iranian leader from Tehran, and Grand Ayatollah Jahni, himself.

"You seem to be a little short on ayatollahs, Jahni."

"Just the Grand ones. I am the last. We have plenty of clerics. We can make more."

"That won't be necessary. Here." He motioned.

They stepped out onto a balcony.

Arrayed before them was the entire citizenry of Persepolis, plus the neighboring populations.

Rusty stepped up to the microphone.

He raised his hands, responding to the deafening applause. "It's finally done! Persia is once again." His words transformed as he spoke, from the Persian into several foreign languages, each assigned to a set of speakers with the specific language stenciled on their sides. "2,336 years ago we lost our lands, one of the greatest empires in history. 2,336 years. To the day. The believers of the Zoroastrian faith were persecuted. That persecution ends today!"

His words elicited yells from the crowd and shaking of fists.

"Persecute the Muslims!"

"Persecute the Arabs!"

Once again, Rusty held his hands aloft. Accompanied by the shaking of his head. "No, my brethren. For now and for eternity, we take the moral high ground. Never to relinquish."

The Grand Ayatollah took a step toward Rusty, who quickly interpreted the man's intent. He stepped to one side as Jahni enlightened the crowd.

"This is a new time. Peace is breaking out." He paused. "In the Middle East."

Cheers embraced the crowd of nearly 200,000.

"It's time for us to do one thing. We must picture, in our mind's eye, the One God. He watches. He sees us fight, and kill each other. And he says, "No! No! No!"

He surveyed the crowd. The now silent crowd. A quick glance at Rustom Modi. He continued.

"Remember this. Tolerance of all beliefs. The Zoros believe what they do and have for many centuries. Love thy neighbor is not an option. It is a requirement. Above all, we must make our Creator smile. If what we do will make him smile, we are on the right track. I personally witnessed these thoughts as they were presented to the religious leaders of all countries of the region. An American, Magus Crayle, put our minds all in the same direction. President Modi and I have talked. We will work to make the new Persia. We shall see … no … we shall guarantee the acceptance and equal, fair treatment. Zoros and Muslims. Equals."

He stepped back to tepid applause.

Modi returned.

"He's right. We shall lead forward."

Then, something unexpected.

"I have a surprise." He turned to the stage entry.

In walked a man they both knew. Quite well.

The newly minted Director of Central Intelligence.

Magus Crayle.

CHAPTER 50

Oblivious to what was occurring in the Middle East, the Pope had been a fan of rock star Jimi Hendrix back to when the iconic musician was still alive. He'd even checked into some history about the guitar slinger. It seemed that Hendrix had two members in his band named Randy. He solved the obvious confusion of calling out, "Hey, Randy" by renaming them Randy Texas and Randy California based upon their origins.

His most trusted assistant happened to be Cardinal Randolph from Saint Louis, who'd just stepped into the Pope's chambers.

"Hey, Randy Missouri. Don't bother me. I'm busy."

"Your Holiness! Please! Stop with the video game! We must leave!"

His frustration rapidly approaching a boiling point, the pope frantically stabbed at the screen image on his Holy tablet.

"With respect," said the cardinal from St. Louis. "What you were about to say … isn't Holy …"

"There!" the Pontiff called out in victory.

Roman Catholicism's top cleric handed over the device. "I'll continue at the next higher level on the jet. I can't wait to utilize our new Wi-Fi system."

"Our new $100,000 communication facility should be quite adequate, Your Eminence."

"I need a nap." With that, the holiest Roman Catholic leaned onto his table and fell asleep.

His peaceful slumber lasted for twenty minutes.

The Pope awoke to his cardinal standing three feet away, awaiting this very moment. The incessant man spoke as the Pope cleared his eyes.

"To attend the next meeting, the C Summit, you must follow certain protocols."

"And if I, Pope of all that is Holy, do not?"

"Then, you would not be allowed in the Summit."

"I choose not to go. How's that?"

"Not an option. The Islam leader and the top Jewish rabbi would then structure, and agree on, the grand peace Mr. Crayle alluded to at the B Summit. You would be seen by the world … as irrelevant. Or worse. Not supportive of the peace."

"Damned if I do, damned if I don't."

"Not to worry. There is only one requirement that is difficult."

"Let me hear."

"All three of you, the Three Kings as you will be billed, must ride into Jerusalem … on donkeys."

The Pope really wanted to get angry, but a mental visual precluded that outcome. He burst into laughter, doubling up, his torso bouncing up and down.

For minutes it lasted. The cardinal thought the leader of the Roman Catholicism's global millions had cracked up.

But, no.

He regained His composure, glancing at the cardinal. "Do I ride the beast from the Vatican to Jerusalem? If so, I better get going. Out of Italy. Across the Balkans. Turkey. Lebanon. Half of Israel."

"Not enough time, I'm afraid,"

Speaking softly now, the cardinal informed him.

The Pope switched back to angry.

"Don't you use vulgarities in my presence!"

His confidant and closest advisor realized the aging man in white had some time ago entered his latter years. He leaned in.

"Holy ship," he said, emphasizing the final percussive.

• • •

In short order, they were out the door and into their latest vehicular donation from the Germans with the Pope blessing everyone in sight on the way to the port city, Civitavecchia. The new pope-mobile sped along, its sing song siren blaring for all to hear.

"I'm infallible, Cardinal, so why wouldn't I beat the damned video game?"

"Now that you've utilized your exalted position to condemn it to damnation, I'm sure your fortunes will improve."

"I'm glad that 'kiss ass' is a figurative term. I'd hate to feel those lips of yours on my butt."

"Figurative. Yes."

"The encounter ahead will be quite draining. I'm going to catch some more shut eye. Okay?"

• • •

In the new Persian capitol, Persepolis, the Grand Ayatollah was ready for lunch.

"I'd like a sandwich, Number Two."

"What sort of sandwich, Number One?" The Iranian second-in-command winked. "A BLT?"

No response. The leader's mind wandered.

He realized one thing. His primary antagonist, known as Magus Crayle, was not only intelligent, but charismatic. The man had gotten inside his head. After his first encounter, he'd totally lost any animus he possessed toward Christians, and even Jews. If he didn't stay away from Mr. Crayle, he'd find himself embracing atheists. Such as the dearly departed Grand Ayatollah, and former leader, Dohreihmi Fahsolah.

And how was he doing with respect to avoidance? Heading off to a new meeting, a C Summit, in Jerusalem. And who was most likely to not only attend, but to facilitate the session? Magus Crayle.

The Ayatollah's head felt ready to spin like the famous movie character, ET. He checked his Mickey Mouse watch.

Regardless of the time of day, he needed to pray. Right now. If ever he required divine guidance, it was now. The fate of the world *did* hang in the balance.

He deployed his prayer rug. Before he could kneel and get serious, Grand Ayatollah Number Two raced in.

"No! No! No!"

Number One acquiesced.

The other man rolled up the rug, tucked it under his arm, and declared, "Gotta go! We're so outta here!"

As his number two hustled him out the door, he had a final thought. It was his assistant's seemingly spurious Americanisms that would have to go.

Other than that, one thing was clear. Why'd Allah not provided him a heads up? And who'd scheduled the successor to the B Summit in Jerusalem? He and the Pope had to travel for hours, while the top Jewish rabbi could just walk down the street.

He shook his head at the unfairness of life, and moved on.

CHAPTER 51

The men, now referred to worldwide as The Three Kings, entered the C Summit facility past guardians Phoebe and Micmac.

They relieved Rabbi-In-Chief Kushner of a six-pointed, martial arts throwing star that dangled from his neck.

The Pope surrendered his Holy Scepter, its long handle serving as a scabbard for a double-edged blade.

The third and final, Grand Ayatollah Jahni, extracted the ceremonial dagger from his waistband.

Thus disarmed, the three Holy men passed through individualized detectors and biometric scanners without further ado.

The room itself had been colored a peaceful light blue. Off-white cloud images adorned the ceiling. The flooring was a medium brown carpet. The feel was that of heaven and earth for the clerics.

Against the walls—left, right, and ahead—sat three wooden boxes, each topped with four clear, vertical Plexiglas sides. Each one nearly as tall as the four foot high boxes supporting them.

On the far side of the Plexiglas, the men noticed a document of sorts. And a religious symbol.

The supreme Israeli rabbi stepped to the one sporting the Star of David. He read the label, which elevated him to a higher level of speechless.

The Christian was drawn to the symbol of the cross. He stopped. And read.

Last, because he was quite wary of the other two, Grand Ayatollah Jahni took the one with the crescent moon and star that remained. He read the label. He gasped.

The Jew collected himself first. "It … it is the … the first Torah!"

"Mine is the initial Holy Bible!"

"And mine, the first Qur'an!"

The door opened behind them. They heard it, but couldn't take their eyes off the visual religious feast just inches away.

They recognized the voice.

"Good morning, gentlemen. Let me answer the obvious question. The documents before you are quite real. They've been carefully and thoroughly vetted. Carbon-dated to the correct periods, and reviewed by our CIA scholars. Yes, they are real. And, yes, you may have them."

"With this setup, we can't even examine them," said the rabbi.

"We can't touch them," followed the ayatollah.

An epiphany struck the remaining cleric. "We've seen the carrots, Mr. Crayle. Now, where is the stick?"

"It is quite simple, and should not after our last meet surprise you."

The three were not at all sure of what was transpiring. They each remembered what happened not too many days before. How they'd been duped into attending that B Summit meeting in Casablanca. How compromising photos had been used by this man and associates to extort desired future behaviors from them.

The American, Magus Crayle, at the behest of American President Kimbel Stones, had precipitated the entire event.

It was why they were here now. In Jerusalem. Likely for the final time. Why? They didn't know.

Would they see Mr. Crayle again after this? They didn't know that, either.

Did they have any choice in the matter?

No.

Of this, they were sure.

CHAPTER 52

"And now, I need to conduct private sessions with each of you. Your three religions have common needs that I've outlined, but there are unique needs for each that are better discussed in private. So, Rabbi Kushner. Remain seated."

The other clerics glanced at each other, and then at the Jew. They stood, filing out the door into the ante-room. With Phoebe and Micmac.

Assured that the door clicked shut, Crayle addressed the Israeli.

"Please, Rabbi. There is no way to achieve what we must as long as violence looms. You have a special situation where the same piece of land possesses two legitimate claimants. The Israeli Jews and the Palestinians."

"This is quite well known. It does not require privacy."

"What you are about to do does require privacy. You must make their top cleric an offer he can't refuse."

The rabbi drew a mental picture of that notion from the movie, The Godfather. He noted the inclusion of the elements, God and father, but quickly chased the notion from his mind. He knew he needed to maintain full focus.

Crayle continued.

"The state of Israel will transition into the Holy Land. A proclamation shall be announced that the One God so talked about over the millennia demands it. That way, it's not a Jewish notion. It's a universal notion. All who support this notion of peace for all shall be invited in. All who persist with violence will be punished and exiled. There will be no second chances for them. A place will be found, by the way, for the exiles. It shall have the prime characteristic of the legendary Hotel California. Likely, an island. The occurrences of recidivism with respect to said violence will, by definition, be zero. The peoples of the Holy Land shall finally live in peace. We must assure—meaning the three of you—that any clerics who do not preach peace for all will likewise be condemned to the island."

The Rabbi nodded in agreement. "The Island of the Damned, it shall be. It sounds like a movie title."

"It probably is. And there's more. All citizens of the Holy Land must be treated equally. There are items known as unalienable human rights that accrue to all equally."

"Codified in the American Constitution, if I remember correctly."

"Not every one. The right to defend oneself and one's property is an inherent right so obvious it is not spelled out. That there are rights not enumerated in our document has mention."

"There is more?"

"Borders must be respected. The Holy Land shall have the borders with surrounding countries at the extremes of today's Israel and Palestinian Territories."

"Must there be religious police?"

"No. All people will have the aspects of religious beliefs available to learn. Whether and how they follow them will be up to them, short of outright criminal activity. You, and the other two Kings, shall indicate that the so-called One God you all agree exists and that you preach to, must make the final reckoning. It is not for human kind to do."

"In other words, Mr. Crayle, it's not for us to usurp … from the One God."

Crayle handed the Rabbi a phone. "This is of a matched pair. You. Me. All comms between us shall be encrypted and decrypted by these devices. Your security code …" He supplied a scripture reference. "Fifteenth word. By the way, I'd originally considered using a romance novel."

The Rabbi caught the dig. Romance not to be a cherished trait for a society that covered up its women.

Crayle gave an eyebrows raised "Question?" glance.

"We'll stay in touch as needed, then."

"At least once per week. Until we're on a roll. I expect momentum to pick up. You will see happenings and pronouncements along the way and know that they play to the overall theme of peace for the planet."

"Good. Then we're done … for the day?"

"Please exit and wait there. For security sake, and for other reasons that will become obvious, you three will leave together. Uh, send in the Grand Ayatollah."

Jahni entered the room shortly after the Rabbi departed.

Crayle motioned him to sit down. He repeated the generalities from the previous meeting. Then, he added the specifics.

"The absence of violence must extend to women. No beatings. No stonings. No shaving of heads to demean for misbehaviors. And, the most difficult, the Holy Lands must treat men and women with equal respect."

"Mr. Crayle, you can't undo hundreds of years of built-in religious culture with a wave of your hand."

"This is a practical matter. We don't know who will cure cancer. Or other severe diseases. The only one who does know is the One God everyone now talks about. And it has never been indicated to us mere mortals what the gender of that life saving individual will be.

We must see that all doors are opened, so that the one chosen by this Creator can walk through. Don't you agree?"

Jahni didn't have to think long on that one. "All doors open. I will do my part."

"You are correct in one aspect. It is not always best to slam people with such a notion. One method would be to recognize women who, in history as well as today, have stepped out of the traditional role, and have helped all of society with their accomplishments. Madame Curie comes to mind. World renowned physicist and chemist. Two Nobel prizes, as I recall."

"If I may, I want to fabricate a solution regarding the Muslim female, and attitudes toward non-Muslim females, then discuss it with you before implementing. Is that possible?"

"You are getting the systems methodology, Jahni." Crayle smiled, and handed the cleric a special phone. "To that end, here is the mate to one I have. Specifically, just you and me. And here …" He handed him a yellow post-it. "… is the security password. It is reference to a specific verse in the Qur'an, the fifteenth word."

"And these phones are safe from interception?"

"The comms traffic on these is heavily encrypted. Prime number-based encryption. Only divisible by one and itself. The longer, the more secure. Would you like for me to go into greater detail?"

In anticipation of a serious Tylenol moment, Jahni shook his head.

"I'll take your word."

Crayle slid a covered serving tray down the Table of the Last Supper.

The Grand Ayatollah lifted the lid.

The aroma brought a brief smile.

He stared at the single strip of cooked bacon before partaking of the tainted flesh.

"Mmmm."

"We're good, then?"

"Yes. Good."

With that, Crayle shook the man's hand, directed him outside, and then asked the remaining of the Three Kings to enter.

In short order, the Pope sat at the Table of the Last Supper along with the CIA's new DCI and World Peace proponent.

"First off, Your Eminence, you must focus on peace for all of human kind. Especially in your addresses to the square below your Vatican apartments. Always. Finish your speeches, every one, with those two words. World peace. The more lips we have them on, the sooner we arrive at our goal."

"I could, you know, refuse. You can't blackmail me for eating pork. It is not forbidden in my religion."

"Point taken. However, your aspect of the global religious schema might take a drubbing if I produced absolute proof that your predecessor … was an atheist. Hmmm?"

"I will do as you say. Are we finished?"

"There's more. I will need you to do something symbolic to match what the Rabbi and Grand Ayatollah have done. They ate the pork. Specifically, bacon. Since that is not forbidden in your religion, what do you suggest to signify your commitment?"

"It so happens that I love pork. And bacon is my favorite. If I pass on that to indicate my dedication to the cause, that should be sufficient."

It sounded good. But, unknown to Crayle, he'd already arranged with the Cardinal to feast on a BLT when he returned to the Vatican. He almost laughed at the memory. His oft humorous number two even promised to transport avocados all the way from California for some Holy Guacamole. And, best yet, no one, not even the CIA man before him, knew.

"Oh. By the way, Your Eminence. I know about the avocados. And the BLT."

"But—"

"No bacon."

"If I do … in a moment of weakness … I shall confess my sin."

"To whom?"

"Uh …"

"No bacon."

Crayle waited for any more diatribe and heard none. He gave the man a special phone with similar instructions as the other two, shook the Pope's hand, and showed him out.

• • •

There. It was over. The C Summit was in the books.

Crayle thanked the three religious leaders one final time. Micmac and Phoebe returned their weapons, and escorted them out of the Hall of the Last Supper.

No one noticed Crayle as he said farewell to the MacKays, and slipped out the back way. Hekka awaited in a special rental vehicle. A warm kiss later, and they were off. Not to the airport as one would expect. Rather, a special place. Fully arranged by their off-the-books travel agent from his secret lair in Nova Scotia, Darryl.

But Hekka wasn't alone. The presence of a second individual indicated that Alona was somewhere in the vicinity. Probably now tracking down Lenny for an active plane ride home.

With the seat belt buzzer forecasting an impending doom, he slid into the back seat to free little Kianna from her protective cocoon seat, and just hold her for a while.

• • •

The Three Kings, once outside the Hall, mounted their respective donkeys, earlier retrieved from that special Bethlehem manger. The wranglers led them through a jam packed Via Dolorosa, providing a degree of discomfort to the Pope. It seemed that Jesus had dragged his cross past the fourteen stations along this very street. This gave him pause. Was it time to call in the Calvary?

The Pope, leader of all who are Catholic, laughed at his ridiculous play on words.

Along the route, smiling happy people wished the three well. They waved signs in all languages proclaiming WORLD PEACE.

After what seemed an hour, the trio arrived at the airport, dismounted their rides, waved to the throng, said their goodbyes, and boarded their private jet rides home. All except the Rabbi. He hopped into a brand new stretch BMW, heading to his abode a short distance away.

Hours passed before Grand Ayatollah Jahni arrived at the airport for Persepolis ready to pick up the pieces, and along with the new leader, Rustom Modi, contribute to a peaceful Persia.

The Pope touched down at the Rome airport a couple of hours later, hopped into a spanking new Mercedes Pope mobile, and was home asleep at the Vatican a short time later.

Exhausted from the trip, he hadn't even noticed his new ride's license plate.

WORLD PEACE.

In Latin.

CHAPTER 53

With the C Summit concluded, Magus and Hekka Crayle opted for a little R & R.

As typical with the obsessive planner, he had it all designed in as a 'post mission wind down' and didn't share the itinerary until they arrived at the shore.

When their Mossad-supplied driver departed, they prepared for the necessary rest and relaxation that had become rest and rehabilitation at this point. Crayle led them to the dock.

"This is it." He pointed. "The vendor described this row boat to me as a modern, fabricated, replica of an actual boat carbon-dated to the Jesus period. It'd even been labeled The Jesus Boat.

They climbed in. An attendant pushed them free of the beach.

Baby Kianna rocked to sleep before the Crayles had rowed 100 yards from shore. They stowed the oars for a bit while he checked the Holy Bible he'd been gifted by the Pope to see if it indicated the best fishing spot on the Sea of Galilee.

As the two focused on the scriptures, they didn't notice Kianna had returned to the land of the awake.

"Bird!" she cried out.

Her parents' heads spun in the direction their daughter pointed.

There, in the distance, about fifty feet off the water's surface came a drone. Right toward them.

Quick, both accessed their sidearms, whipping them in the direction of the threat.

The airborne craft not only approached directly toward them, but gradually decreased altitude.

But they didn't shoot. The drone had popped a flag they recognized as an American flag. Then, that flag disappeared to be replaced by one both recognized immediately. The CIA seal. They lowered their weapons.

When the drone arrived, it hovered. A line lowered a bucket. An ice bucket. Containing a bottle of champagne. And a note.

"Congrats on the pregnancy!"

Signed by K. Stones and J. Sommers.

Jaws dropped. "We are? How …"

They didn't even know.

• • •

"Only one fishing rod and reel, Hekka. What to do?"

"How about this? You concentrate on fishing. I'll reminisce our ultra-romantic past."

Before Crayle could react further, Hekka was in his arms. With an arm wrap, and a serious kiss.

When she finally backed off, she bore more than her trademark, minimalist smile.

"That was good. But what if Jack and his resources are wrong? What if there's no pregnancy?"

"That would just mean that there's no pregnancy yet."

Unlike her, she waved her arms this way and that, as her mind relived the past.

"Not in any order, here goes.

Monte Carlo nuke. Patti's doing. Took out the Illuminé top dog, the Elder, who was also the Monaco Prince. Oh, yes. And Doctor Monika Rikki.

The Xinjiang nuke at Ürümqi. Collected the Communist leadership in Beijing for the big takedown.

The Marseille nuke. Congregated the French leadership to Paris. Almost got them, too.

Paris nuke almost worked. A little nighttime work by the team in the Eiffel Tower with New Year's Eve fireworks and a lightning storm all at once to add a little fun to the op.

The initial nuke, in central Iran. Showed what Lalumière could do with one of those CIA Universal Remote controls.

Beijing. One of Chin's nukes in the underground city. There goes the leadership.

Mini-nuke bomb factory in China. Took out the whole design and manufacturing team.

Anastasia's Moscow nuke. Took out the remnants of the Communist Party there. And rendered the remains of the two Vladimirs into vapor.

Marching air blast mini-nukes headed from Los Angeles toward our home in Big Bear. A close one. Escape to Temecula. Who would've thought.

The Stuka nuke at Xian that took out new emperor, Chin Yao-wu, and the Iranian nuclear bomb physicist.

Puerto Montt, Chile. Bomb blew up the Nuncio's plane headed back to the Vatican. Another aimed at the volcano chain tried to set them all off.

Lenny over the Middle East nearly self-sacrificing to destroy the rogue Grand Ayatollah's targeting of Mecca. To blame Israel.

Australia's Red Center. Three bombs. Three babies.

The New Zealand nuke set to take out the Kiwi and Aussie rugby teams, and most of Auckland. Saved again by Lenny.

The Aussie Illuminé chief died. You did that at the reef.

Vlad, before being desecrated in Moscow by the Czarina, died of Novichok poisoning.

Iran leader, Grand Ayatollah Dohreihmi Fahsolah. Stabbed by the other top clerics in his Caesar Forum replica under Tehran.

Sylvain killed by Pattie right after his coronation. Lifelong dream … caput.

Pattie died. Of a broken heart. I and my ten-inch Bowie knife will have to take credit for that one.

Neil Wohlford. One time head of the CIA's off-the-books Strategic Solutions Office. Jack's boss. A member of a long list. Dead at Pattie's hand.

The Ottos of Germany. The Aryan Alliance. All taken down.

General Li. The man who killed your father over in Hong Kong during the Vietnam War. Down, with extreme prejudice, by my one and only. Now, that was justice.

Last, there was the recent rescue of Lenny and Phoebe, who we all were absolutely sure, were dead. Nicely done, Mag.

Oh, yes. And the Summits. The notion of World Peace.

She drew a breath.

"Whew!"

He could tell she was finished. "That's quite a memory."

She gave him the smile.

Something grabbed her attention.

"Oh, look, Mag. My exuberance rocked the boat. Our baby's rocked back to sleep."

"And … "

"I know what to do. Let's assure that Jack's right. Right here. Right now."

"You have got to be kidding. Out here in the middle of the Sea of Galilee? Out in the open? In the Holy Land?"

"I've got this, my wonderful husband. Every now and then I'll call out the Lord's name. Surely, he will bless us with our second child."

She settled into the bottom of the boat.

Crayle scanned for witnesses, and reassured himself Jack's drone was gone.

He threw up his hands in surrender, and joined her. With only a few last words.

"The things I do for God and country."

• • •

Just one red eye flight later, the Crayle family was re-ensconced in the tidy and calm resort community they called home. Big Bear.

The three of them got some necessary sleep.

• • •

Mag Crayle rose early the next morning at his Fawnskin cabin. Before Hekka and Kianna. His frosted bedroom window indicated it was cold outside.

Resolute, he donned heavy black Levi's over his black silk thermal underwear. He garnished the outfit with an old foul-weather jacket in Army olive drab—thanks to his father, and a matching knitted wool watch cap pulled down over his ears. He finished with Nam-era jungle boots atop the appropriate government issue socks. He took a moment to glance at a spray bottle of suntan lotion, knowing that somewhere in the world, there existed warmth and sunshine.

A stop at the hall closet for his fishing gear and, still in stealth mode, he stole out the back sliding door, dropping neither rod and reel nor tackle box in the process. Such early success portended a very good day.

That's when the bushy-tailed squirrel dashed across just mere feet away.

He stopped.

His feet didn't.

Splat!

What does one do after an unceremonious pratfall? Scan for witnesses.

None.

Good.

Up on his feet, he collected his stuff, and plodded through the previous night's snowfall the fifty feet to his private dock his cabin shared with the Jack Sommers' Big House.

The surface of Southern California's Big Bear Lake, at 6,827 feet above sea level, appeared speckled with plates of broken ice, from one foot to several feet in diameter. He'd rely on his heretofore latent casting skills to drop his hook into the micro-narrow wet divides between the ice patties.

No sooner had he sat himself down on the dock's edge, feeling the solitude, than he heard noises from behind.

He spun.

Here came Mick MacKay, known to friends and associates as Micmac, running his way at a steady jog.

"What have you got there?" Crayle called at the former Navy SEAL.

"I've got the old Vietnam-era red Frisbee … and some flippers." He smirked as he pulled up next to his friend, and fellow spy. He didn't need to mention the flat-screen TV monitor, plus a pillow to serve as a seat cushion.

"Two pair?"

Crayle glanced back and forth at the icy cold water.

"I thought we'd play some Frisbee."

"In the lake?" The word Incredulous didn't capture his look.

"Never too cold, or too hot, for a SEAL. We can watch TV to warm up."

Crayle considered the latter. He wondered how a lobster felt when plopped into boiling water. A thought for another time.

Micmac flipped on the TV.

A motorboat on the lake interrupted their repartee. They turned toward the sound.

At a distance of about 200 feet, an aluminum-hulled craft motored into view, gingerly pushing ice blocks aside. One person operated an outboard. The second, near the bow, stood and held a double-barreled shotgun.

Crayle pondered out loud. "Bird season?"

"Uh, no," came the reply.

The gunman tracked his firearm high in the sky as if preparing to shoot. Then, dropped the barrel to point at the shocked onlookers on the dock.

Micmac, known to the CIA's Science and Technology Directorate as code name Gadget Man, had performed a few, slight modifications to the Frisbee.

He dropped the fins, pressed hard on the top and bottom of the recreational disc, then flung it toward the boat.

It flew out, then angled downward.

The gunman tried to track it, preparing to fire.

But the spinning device skipped off the lake's surface, and angled left.

The assassin smiled. He drew down on his target. Puzzled, he saw Crayle and Micmac leaning to their right, his left.

A sudden breeze seemed to have caught the Frisbee, changing its course in the direction of their lean. The lean appeared to be some sort of flight control.

The Micmac-modified object homed in on the boat, striking it amidships.

Boom!

The ball of flame instantly reached a still uncapped gas can.

Adding fuel to the fire.

Crayle realized it was all a simulation. Another installment of the latest Artificial Intelligence mayhem coming from the S & T Directorate.

The former SEAL switched off the monitor, and turned to his friend and cohort.

"Tell me, Mag. Tell me about your very first gig. You know. As a spy."

"You've heard the details. I was at The Farm in Virginia learning tradecraft. And being assessed."

"High marks?"

"So they said. But the instructors never showed us anything in writing."

"Any take a liking to you?"

"One did. Name was Sal. For Sally."

"Last name?"

Crayle laughed. "I asked. I was in spy mode by then. I knew she couldn't tell me. I wanted to check her reaction to the question. We'd just completed a class in interpreting body language."

"And …"

"She was the embodiment of a female United Fighting Championship champion. Very tight body. Close cropped blonde hair. Maybe five-five. Didn't smile much. When she did, it meant something." He waited. "She smiled."

"Sounds like the two of you spent some closet time."

"Against the rules. And the answer is Yes. I figured she was teaching me that, at the base level, there are rules, but above that, there are no rules."

"Last name?"

"A place she said she'd always wanted to go. Manila."

Micmac was not just a heavy duty SEAL. He was perceptive. "Sal Manila."

He grabbed the pillow to enact his revenge.

Crayle jumped up, grabbed his gear, and ran.

CHAPTER 54

Their day done, Crayle and Micmac plodded away from the fishing dock toward the cabin with their catch. Their look told anyone watching of success beyond their imagination.

Having trudged the requisite fifty feet from the dock, Crayle and Micmac walked in on Hekka.

Due to the absence of relevant sounds, it appeared that Kianna was down for a nap. The only other person in the cabin was Hekka. She seemed relaxed and pensive as she sat at the dining room table staring at the present given her by the Uzbek, Aziza, before they said their goodbyes in Kashgar.

Crayle agreed wholeheartedly with the relaxation notion.

"Hey, Micmac. How about sticking around for a beer? Local. Celebrate our catch?"

"Local? I don't drink Budweiser."

"Newcastle?"

"Hmmm. Brown beer is good. But I have to get back. Our cupboards are bare. Phoebe wants me along for some replenishment shopping. You know. Take our son along for bonding at the grocery store."

"Alright. See you next week."

"Check."

He let himself out.

Crayle heard the car start up and drive away. He wondered how Micmac—former SEAL, underwater demolitions and weapons expert—would survive the dead fish smell now invading Phoebe's Porsche.

He took a seat at the table.

"Aziza gave it to me in Kashgar. It was at her place. It may have religious value. Such as an icon."

Her comment drew Crayle's mind to a factoid that'd gotten lost in all the action over the past three years. "You know, I've never seen you with a religious book. Where do you keep your Serrano bible?"

"There is no physical book to place on a mantle. Or to tote. You carry yours in here." She held out a cupped hand. "We carry ours in here." She pressed her hand against her heart.

He glanced over at her. She now held her fist closed, so she could regard her finger nails.

"I'm not going to win this, am I?"

Hekka's characteristic, minimalist smile crept onto her lips.

He looked away.

"See how it is. You spend a day or so with Lenny on a trip, and your sense of humor heads due South."

"Our diminutive P.I. associate is infectious."

"The appropriate word is contagious."

Their repartee, itself, headed South. In walked Lenny.

"Yeah, I'm a regular fun-demic. Or is it … pun-demic." He laughed. "I could go global if I'm not stopped." He laughed again. Briefly.

Apparently attempting to track down her errant husband, Phoebe strode into the room, her right hand resting firmly on her holstered

Glock 30. "And with you on your comedy tour, who shall take on the burdensome task of defending the good people of the world?" She received no response. "*C'est moi*! The Lenny vaccine has arrived! *C'est arrivée*! Forty-five caliber, too! Uh … *aussi*!"

Hekka beat her husband to the quandary punch. "French?"

"Been working with ole Doc Rorschach. Three visits, and I'm fluent."

With repartee pretty much exhausted, Phoebe led Lenny back out to their rides, and they departed.

Finally alone, Crayle and Hekka focused on her prize surprise from the trip.

"Are you going to open it?"

"Aziza said not until I'm back home. Here goes."

She pulled the tape binding the beautiful red, blue, green, and yellow ancient silk wrapping the artifact. That kept the nature of the item secret except for its noticeable heft.

"Paper was an extremely important Central Asian commodity in ancient times. It was even used to embalm bodies. Whoever bound this cut strips of it the width of the tape."

"That allows the tape's adhesive to bind and exert pressure. Without the glue damaging the silk."

"Nicely deduced."

Finished with the tape strips, she carefully unwrapped the silk.

There before them sat a carved wooden icon from times of yore.

The carving depicted a family of four. A man, a woman, and a young boy and girl. All dressed in clothes fabricated from animal skins. Both the woman and girl wore long, black hair. The males sported shoulder length hair of the same color.

"He's carrying a bow and arrow."

"Yes. And the arrows appear to be from the same bird as my ancestors."

"The artist who crafted this captured the flesh tone, Hekka."

"Oh, my. There's the reddish hue of my ancestors."

Crayle noticed the engraved letters beneath the scene. And sat back.

"It's a word," Hekka concluded. "Spelled C-E-P-P-A-H-O." She pronounced it, *sep-pah-hoe*.

"Seppahoe?"

"It sounds like something from my Takic language."

"Unless it's Cyrillic."

"You mean, as in Russian?"

"Yes."

"Well, Aziza told me there were Russian speakers in the Stans. That would explain the presence of that alphabet." She glanced his way, knowing there was more.

Crayle grinned.

"You want me to pronounce it?"

Her look pretended she was considering the possibility.

"Ten. Nine. Eight ..."

"SERRANO!"

EPILOGUE

A great deal happened in a short period of time. The answer to *what can one person do* began to take form as the world transitioned. The notion that humanity could take more than 200,000 years to realize that killing each other, in either large or small numbers, was not the answer. Religions created and endured for millennia to point out the obvious and lead the way to peace for all had been ineffective. Some had even contributed to the death and destruction. Now, the opportunity to right the ship was placed on their doorstep. The question arose, would they be up to the task.

The consequence of Hekka's quest across Central Asia and the revamping of the Middle East that traced back to Magus Crayle's activities seemed irreversible.

Still, there were significant impacts and responses from the various people's directly involved.

The Chinese

It finally happened. Ling An-yee, the 21-year-old Empress of China, connected. At the other end, America's newly minted Director of Central Intelligence.

"Mr. Crayle? Uh, Director Crayle?"

"You're trying too hard, Ling. It's Magus."

"I want to portray respect. To your wife. For your new, exalted position. Yes. Respect."

"I know you'll respect my marriage. And thank you, by the way, for the tremendous degree of assistance you provided Hekka on her quest. You'll find that her gratitude is endless."

"Yes. She said. When she stopped by my palace on her way home."

"I wanted to say this to you. Going forward, I'm here to help within the confines of my home country focus. I'm here if you feel the need. Continue to use this special one-to-one, encrypted system as you just did."

"Thank you for that open-ended offer. I'm getting tremendous support for the stability, continued economic prosperity, and my exit from the imperialist attitudes of the past."

"Well, if you get any more fancy ideas, such as the independence of Xinjiang, give me a call."

"By the way, Hekka's speech in Ürümqi, on my behalf, was fantastic. It far exceeded what I or anyone else could do. Her diverse heritage brought credibility. My Chinese defense forces, in Xinjiang for centuries, have been withdrawn to the new border. But ready to assist should opportunists show their hand."

"Your intel agency, now the Ministry of Imperial Security, will help you stay informed. And, oh, we know what they know."

"Is there anything that you don't know?"

"If something comes to mind, I'll call."

"Like me converting our military's South China Sea islands into a Disneyland? Children from all over can come there to celebrate your new global peace? First in the region, then in the world?"

"You continue to amaze me, Ling."

"Oops. Got to go, Magus. Our baby emperor needs a change."

" 'Til next time."

He clicked off.

The Germans

The subset of Germans call themselves the Aryan Alliance. They pointed at filth and disorder brought into their country by non-Germanic immigrants, and ignored the benefits such as cheap labor and alternative ways of doing things.

They also ignored that the Hitler term, Aryan, included a swath of humanity that ranged South through the Balkans and into modern Persia.

Crayle's major worry was not as much their rising influence in German or international politics as it was the intel he'd obtained in the recent Iberian operation with his six member team. The perpetrators, a Spaniard and a Portuguese, had contracted with the AA to secretly bore a cross-peninsula tunnel in return for a spare, mini-nuke warhead.

Added to that, the natural connection of the Alliance to the German-inspired Illuminati of old that could easily tie them to the Illuminé offshoot that'd been Crayle's nemesis for the past several years.

It seemed simple.

As DCI, he'd dispatch a covert team to locate and neutralize the bomb.

Unfortunately, the best team for the job, with its three years of direct experience, and 100% success rate, was home for good.

Done.

Surely, the sitting DCI couldn't revitalize his crew, and sneak off and get the job done anywhere in the world.

But, a successful op in Germany would still leave one final miniaturized nuclear Made In China device out there.

That would be the one still held by the new president of Persia.

Rustom Modi.

The French

As beautiful and idyllic as Versailles was, early Winter brought a distinct chill to it. Jean-Marc Lalumière, officially King Louis XX, stared out over the grounds past the grand fountain.

"Come to bed," came from behind. His wife, and current Queen of Sweden, toyed with her negligee. "We'll make one or more heirs to the throne."

"I just received the title. I want to enjoy it before thinking about giving it up some day."

"Ah. My English is too accented. How about, *Voulez-vous coucher avec moi se soir?*"

Jean-Marc tried to ignore her request.

"We shall enjoy what we have for now."

"We? I don't see my input being considered."

"It is the royal plural." He turned, poking his finger at his chest. "We means me."

She performed the raised eyebrows for effect, and nodded agreement. The queen of all that was France and Sweden dropped her negligee to the floor.

The new King Louis pushed his lips to one side.

"Then, there's that," he said.

The Swedes

The Swedes seemed to have misplaced their queen. Actually, she now resided in sumptuous comfort in the Palace of Versailles with French King Louis XX.

The Nordic makeup was quite the opposite of the French, taken collectively, but the Swedes hoped to bridge the gap by co-developing a new dish. Lingonberry Soufflé.

The push back from their across-the-waters neighbor was a simple, "We don't require assistance cooking anything."

Undaunted, the Swedes created a commission to study the differences.

Aside from that conflict, they saw no other near or long term threats to their country. The Germans consumed all their energies with internal politics. History had taught the French never to attack anyone. The rest of Europe was likewise benign.

The sole potential threat, which it had been for several centuries, was Russia. Its military could quickly deploy from Murmansk near the North Cape above Scandinavia, and it would be hard, if not impossible, to hold at bay.

Fortunately, its new leader, Czarina Anastasia, spent most of her time in the bedroom in Catherine's Palace, and had little left for imperialistic exploits.

A good sign would be for Russia to exit eastern Ukraine and the Crimea. Outwardly neutral Sweden would deploy its own espionage and special operations resources to that end.

The Vatican

The Pope glared at the sandwich. His sworn enemies like the Devil himself never posed the least of such temptation. A BLT, no less. Its aroma targeting him, he was certain. Yes. There is a Devil.

"World Peace," came the voice of his number one. Cardinal Randy St. Louis almost stated it as a question.

The Pope's consternation was evident. "It's this damned sandwich that stands between humanity and an enduring, pan-global peace."

"If you take a bite, humanity is doomed."

"What to do? My favorite among all foods."

"I can help."

The Cardinal reached past his superior, retrieved the demon sandwich, and took a mouthful.

The Pope's jaw didn't miss hitting the floor by much.

"You … you …"

"There's a reason I wear red," said the Cardinal as he took another gargantuan bite.

"The Devil! It's you!" cried the pontiff. He spun around.

The Cardinal, and the BLT, were gone.

Then, just like that, he returned.

"Had to brush my teeth. You know, I can see why you suspect the Devil of creating the bacon. It was soooo good."

"You are insufferable. And where's the dip you promised? From California? The Holy Guacamole?"

The Cardinal didn't respond. He'd eaten that, too. He quickly switched back to the original subject.

"As Mr. Crayle told you at the C Summit. If foregoing the temptation of bacon means world peace, don't succumb to it."

"How … how in Hell do you know what he said? In private? At the summit? We were alone. With sound and technology protection. You … oh, my God … you're an asset! A spy!"

The Cardinal lowered himself to his knees.

"Your Eminence. I have a confession."

The Americans

The Crayle team—all three couples, each with a baby—congregated, as requested, in the covert Cathedral some 300 feet underground in the District of Columbia. The children were instantly in awe of the vertical, stained glass windows. The same windows their parents had witnessed during their weddings. The light through the stained glass would've inspired. Except all of the adults knew it was fake.

Fake?

In Washington, D.C.?

Who would've thought?

A man they knew quite well stepped before them along with a familiar blonde and brunette.

"Hey, team. Susanna has agreed to be my wife! And Luisa, my mistress!"

Stones, President of all that was the United States, thought that was funny. And laughed.

Susanna, cool as always, glanced up at him, and said but two words.

"Mossad."

And then.

"Kidon."

The president, well aware of the Israeli spy agency, and its assassination subset, finished the thought with, "Enough said."

Crayle surmised. "I believe she'll keep him on the straight and narrow. I propose a toast." He hefted an imaginary glass.

"And let their love be forever!"

Out from the shadows stepped another easily recognized soul.

The Pope.

Clearly, he would perform for President Stones and Susanna the anticipated Christian ritual.

Not yet.

Behind him entered two they didn't expect.

"I'll perform the intros," Stone said. "This is Rabbi Kushner from Israel, and next to him, the Grand Ayatollah Jahni. They stopped by. I thought, " 'What the hey.' "

The Crayles

The pair, Hekka and Magus, were at long last enjoying the peace and quiet of their Big Bear cabin.

Baby Kianna lay in her basinet fast asleep. She and her parents were finally alone as a family. The friends and allies had gone home. Crayle glanced into his wife's eyes.

"Well, we've done it again. For the final time. We need a break."

Hekka took a peek at her vibrating Smartphone. "This just in. It seems *your* phone was unavailable. They're ready for you."

"For what?"

"DCI. It says, you start Monday."

He wasn't finished.

She had known him, in all senses of the word, long enough to read his expression.

"What?"

"Oh, nothing."

She deployed her hands and fingers in the *GIVE* configuration.

"I've got an idea for another novel."

The Israelis

Back at his workspace in Jerusalem, Rabbi Kushner envisioned one tough road ahead. Killing each other over the millennia had become a duty for some, a pastime for others. Palestinians and Jews alike.

His brief reverie was abated by his thirty-something assistant bearing gifts. She placed the large, white, oval dinner plate before him.

"Fit for a King." She referenced Judaism's top cleric as one of the Three Kings who attended the recent C Summit. "If a single strip of bacon can start us on the road to World Peace, imagine what this full rack of pork ribs can do."

He finger-tasted the barbeque sauce.

"Honey chipotle," she informed.

His mind drifted. This young Delilah reminded him of his past life. Beginning service in the military just out of school, he was soon recruited into Mossad. He rose to a first-level management job and an assistant had been chosen for him. An attractive, five foot five, perfect figure type. With shoulder length hair died blood red that fell straight down until it curved forward at the bottom. And quite intelligent, to boot.

Her spy agency credentials included Kidon, Mossad's assassination entity.

He'd lost track of her, but later used his agency resources to track her. She'd left the service, and moved across the world to a small, Southern California coastal town. To work at a small newspaper in marketing. Developing killer ads, his mind quipped. A visual showed the same tall, thin facial structure with the red die gone, and her natural blonde bidding welcome.

By some quirk of fate, Susanna now reported directly to American President Stones as his principle speech writer. Since he was no doubt behind all the World Peace crap, she'd become a potential, ideal asset for one Rabbi Kushner.

Just then, five men burst through the door, brandishing curved Saracen period swords, each with its own historical provenance.

The Rabbi flung the razor edge Star Of David that hung from his neck to little avail.

Not to worry.

Delilah had them all down in 2.4 seconds.

He glanced at her. For the young woman, blowing smoke was a non-trivial act. She did so at the end of her silenced weapon.

The Rabbi surveyed the scene.

"World Peace? It'll take some work."

The Uighurs

Arzu sat in the former People's Park in her hometown, and new country's capitol, Ürümqi. The day was peaceful, with a Winter's chill.

Still, thousands of her countrymen milled about, just looking at her as if she were some form of revered statue.

All she'd hoped for, for all her years, was a someday free Xinjiang. That's all. Her interests and talents pushed her toward the intelligence side of things.

Though young, she'd run in secret the Uighur intel operation with a cover job of tour guide. It worked. Its Han Chinese official counterpart, of Beijing's Ministry of State Security, feeling relegated to the far western Xinjiang province as a form of punishment, either never caught on, or didn't really care.

One day changed the whole mix. Ling hadn't apprized her of the upshot of the speech delivered by Hekka. Likely, just a pep talk from the empress. Surely, not an edict of independence for Xinjiang.

When the words escaped from Hekka's lips that the Uighurs were, as of that very moment, a free and independent people, tears had rushed to Arzu's eyes.

The phrase, don't shoot the messenger, referred to bad news. In this case, Hekka delivered good news. She became an instant hero. A statue would be in order.

Her thoughts were interrupted by an old man who approached. Arzu knew him as the patriarch of Ürümqi.

"Forgive me," he said in halting English. "We have a request."

"I'm not in a position to honor or grant any requests. I'm just ..."

She glanced around. The thousands of people were now crowded near, but keeping a respectful twenty feet distant.

The man continued. "We want you to lead us."

Arzu was overwhelmed. Asked to lead the Uighur people.

"Patriarch. I'm only 26."

The Persians

The Grand Ayatollah, leader of Iran, had no options left. The battle was lost.

"You've won. Iran is yours."

"No, my brother. It's ours."

That brought a look of shock to the deposed cleric. He regained enough composure to respond. "Separated at birth. A Muslim father and Zoro mother."

"Perfect. For our purpose."

"We shall drink, then."

The Parsi raised his Kingfisher beer, product of India, brought along just for this occasion.

The Grand Ayatollah raised his non-alcoholic orangina.

The Parsi emitted the toast. "To World Peace."

The other man smiled. "To World Peace."

The End

ABOUT THE AUTHOR

Committed to international affairs, political intrigue, and espionage, novelist Dennis Bowen has researched his stories in more than 75 countries. He engenders realism and spice in his thrillers due to his wartime service, and his defense and intelligence community background, which led one reader to remark, "Bowen knows his stuff." *The Kindred Heritage* follows *The Water Diamonds*, *The Blackstone Perfection*, *The Crystal Seduction*, *The Redrock Quarantine*, *The Final Masquerade*, *The Virtue Transition*, *The Jasmine Negative*, and *The Gospel Labyrinth* as the most recent addition to his International Thriller Series. When not traveling the globe to research his next thriller, he resides on the Southern California coast.

Facebook: http://www.facebook.com/DennisBowenThrillers/
Twitter: http://www.twitter.com/DBowenThrillers/
Website: http://www.dennisbowen.com/

AUTHOR'S NOTE

I hope you enjoyed ***The Kindred Heritage***. As noted on the cover, this is Book 9 of the ***International Thriller Series***. It stands in addition to the original eight-book series. This note explains, in brief, the process I followed from beginning to end. I decided to include it because there are interesting insights for both readers and aspiring authors.

• • •

How did the original sequential series of seven novels come to be? Prior to my initial writing effort, I would go for bicycle rides around a lake. It was a self-imposed prescription for exercise, fresh air, and a mental time out. Ideas for a story would just pop into my head without any solicitation whatsoever. I'd return home and write them in a notebook. By 2011, I decided to write a novel. The plot would demonstrate how the geopolitical landscape could be severely modified by evil-intentioned malefactors using miniature nuclear devices. I decided to write all the stories in long hand to keep myself physically connected, versus the technological mental distancing inherent with using a computer. After substantial scribblings, annotations, and cross-outs, the words did find their way into the digital orchestration.

Notes on the characters, locations, and scenes grew and grew. I attended a few writers' conferences, read several books, and decided to put pen to paper. So I did. My original estimate, however, would produce a novel of about 750 pages. Too big. I divided the story into three successive novels to make it more manageable, and to provide the initial product to readers much faster.

After three months of putting pen to paper, I realized through epiphany that I'd really gotten to know the story, the settings, and the characters. In fact, I knew the latter so well, I could just keep a mental eye on them, and they could write the scenes. The good news was they couldn't charge me for their efforts. And better yet, I could take all the credit.

As I wrote the three novels, ideas kept coming. By the time I finished them, I had enough notes for two more. Okay, I said. It was meant to be a five novel series. By the time I completed the fifth story, I had notes for two more. The trend led me to pronounce, on more than one occasion, the famous line from the Peanuts cartoon series: Charlie Brown saying, "Good grief!" Or words to that effect. At that point, I considered giving up bicycle riding.

As I noted before, a quite knowledgeable individual whose judgment I trust, deeply familiar with the stories and characters, intimated after reading Book 7, *The Jasmine Negative*, that there just might be an eighth novel required. That was Book 8, *The Gospel Labyrinth*. But the characters still were not finished. With ***The Kindred Heritage***, I have extended the eight book series.

Once more. "Good grief!"

• • •

Some, including myself, find that in re-reading any of the ***International Thriller Series*** novels, a reader can enjoy them just as much, or even enjoy them more. You can still get everything in normal, silent reading mode, but I suggest you return to a favorite chapter in this story, read it out loud, visualize the characters and observe the difference.

I do perform a great deal of international research since that is the forum in which my stories take place. Although I plan to finally take a little time off, the ideas never stop coming. Fortunately, I did start a second series I called ***The Backstory Files*** in which I took a second-tier individual from the first series and provided how the title character, ***STONES***, transitioned from a National Security Agency operative to Vice President of the United States in an intense, brief period of time. I have many more characters for which I can write thriller back stories.

And with that, best wishes to all those who've supported my efforts, to all those in foreign lands that have provided precious local flavor intel, and finally to every reader on the entire planet. You are why we do this. Seriously. Thank you.

—Dennis Bowen

www.ingramcontent.com/pod-product-compliance
Lightning Source LLC
Chambersburg PA
CBHW020611310726
48979CB00008B/1427/J

* 9 7 8 1 7 3 6 0 2 6 2 5 0 *